TIME OUT OF MIND

Adria Morris—a name she had picked out of nowhere when she had lost her memory two years ago. She had managed to put her life together—until Kyle Hamilton told her that she bore a remarkable resemblance to someone he once knew . . .

TIME OUT OF MIND

BY
KAY THORPE

MILLS & BOON LIMITED
ETON HOUSE   18–24 PARADISE ROAD
RICHMOND   SURREY TW9 ISR

First published in Great Britain 1987
by Mills & Boon Limited

© Kay Thorpe 1987

Australian copyright 1987
Philippine copyright 1987
This edition 1987

ISBN 0 263 75756 0

Set in Baskerville 10 on 11¼ pt.
01-0887-49524

Computer typeset by SB Datagraphics,
Colchester, Essex

Printed and bound in Great Britain by
Collins, Glasgow

CHAPTER ONE

IF ONLY she could make herself remember. There had been odd flashes from time to time, but nothing concrete; nothing that offered any real hope. To all intents and purposes, her life had begun two years ago on that dingy railway station when she had opened her eyes to find herself facing a metaphorical blank wall.

To have no past was a frightening thing. Even now, her mind found it difficult to accept. Adria Morris was a name chosen at random—the first because it was listed in the book as meaning unknown, the second from a telephone directory. They had placed her age at around twenty-two at the time of her arrival at the hospital, and given her a birthday date of the twenty-ninth of April, which was when she had been found. As good as any, she supposed. It was June again now. Two months into her third year as a new entity. The psychiatrist she still saw on a fortnightly basis had long since given up hope of eliciting any change in her condition; she could sense it from his attitude. Any time now he was going to suggest a cessation of their sessions (a pun in there somewhere) and leave her to make the best of what she had. In many ways it would be almost a relief. Going over and over the same arid ground was a pointless exercise. If she ever did recover her memory it would be because someone or something rewired the burned-out fuse, and after all this time the possibility of that happening was becoming ever more remote. The police had done everything they could. There had even been a newspaper report complete with photograph. But no response. If anyone out there knew who she was they were keeping their own counsel—perhaps with good reason.

Her stop was coming up. She joined those already making their way rearwards along the bus's central aisle, grabbing hold of an overhead strap as brakes were applied. They were running late again; it was almost on the half-hour now, and she still had to get across the road. Jobs weren't so easily come by that she could afford to jeopardise hers by bad time-keeping. Three times already this month, and not yet half-way through it. A lengthy, difficult journey into central London was no real excuse. Few people lived on the store's doorstep. She would simply have to get up half an hour earlier in order to make sure.

There was a promise of heat to come in the silky warmth of the sun when she alighted on to the pavement. The hurrying throng consisted mostly of workers, with a few early shoppers among them, the tourists not yet abroad. Traffic was, as always at this hour, heavy, the gaps few and far between. With the nearest pelican crossing several hundred yards along the road, and time at a premium, it was a case of taking advantage of a temporary slowing of the flow and darting through between two taxi-cabs coasting in the nearside lane.

The sudden screech of brakes hastily applied was followed by the blare of a horn as a large blue saloon pulled up with its bumper almost touching her shin. Adria turned her head and mouthed a silent apology to the man she could see seated at the wheel, noting his frozen expression. Jaywalker though she might be, it was the only way to get where she was going. The traffic had stopped completely now, held up by the lights ahead. She made the far side before the change, quickening her steps in the direction of the familiar solid stone block across the intersection.

It still wanted a whole minute to the half-hour when she

clocked in. That meant her watch was gaining. Probably needed cleaning, she reflected, although at the prices charged by jewellers today it would have to wait a while. At least she could relax right now. That in itself was a comfort.

A couple of the girls greeted her casually in the locker room, continuing with their lively discussion of the previous evening's events as Adria slipped off her cream linen dress and got into the skirt and blouse which constituted the store's uniform. She had formed no close friendships during the eighteen months she had worked here, mostly she was reluctant to have her background—or lack of it—made public property. After one or two overtures had been gently but firmly rebuffed, the others had stopped trying. Adria was aware that she had a reputation for being 'stuck-up', but to her it was the lesser of two evils. All she wanted was to be left alone—at least by people who didn't matter to her. Larry was different. Without him she wasn't sure how she would have managed. He had got her this job, found her a place to live, given her something to hope for at those times when depression and despair had threatened to take over. She was through the worst now, but still grateful. She always would be grateful.

With her blouse buttoned and feet clad in comfortable sandals, she took a comb from her handbag and went to tidy herself at the long mirror running above the half-dozen handbasins. The heart-shaped face within its frame of chestnut hair was familiar enough now, yet she could still recall the utter strangeness of it the first time they had brought her a mirror after her admittance to hospital. Attractive, she had been bound to acknowledge—that at least had been a plus—only it had been like looking at someone else not herself. She hadn't felt like the person revealed in that mirror; she hadn't felt like anyone, if it came to that. In two years she had managed to acquire a certain outer confidence, but underneath she still suffered the same tearing doubt. Who was she? Where did she come from? What had she been doing at Victoria that morning? Mugged, they had said. Hit on the head by some person or persons unknown, and her possessions, if any, stolen. The ladies' cloakroom, that was where they had found her. Beyond that, nothing.

Forget it, she told herself now with wry humour. Look ahead, not back. Perhaps she was better off not knowing in the long run.

The morning got under way. Working on men's toiletries at present, Adria found the mid-week demand limited enough to make time drag a little. She began sorting through stock with a view to getting out her monthly re-ordering list. Tomorrow was her half day, then Friday and then the weekend again. Larry was going to be out of town until the beginning of next week, which meant no shared pub lunch on Sunday. She so much enjoyed their outings, and knew he did, too. Social workers had so many commitments. His job didn't stop at five-thirty or even midnight. Many were the times people phoned him in the early hours just to talk because they couldn't sleep themselves for thinking of their various problems. He didn't seem to mind. Par for the course, he always said.

Someone had paused by the counter. Adria dusted off her hands by brushing them together and turned, the automatic smile abruptly fading as she looked at the man standing there. It had only been a brief glimpse she had had through the car windscreen earlier, but the thick dark hair and tanned lean features were still clearly enough imprinted in her mind's eye to make recognition immediate and unmistakable. He was looking back at her with an odd expression—almost as if he had doubts of his own. Yet his first words served to belie that impression.

'Just checking you're OK,' he said. 'No bruises?'

'Er . . . no.' She was nonplussed, perfectly aware that the near-accident had been entirely her fault. 'It's kind of you to bother,' she added uncomfortably. 'I shouldn't have been crossing the road at all right there and then, only I thought I was late for work and . . .' She broke off, seeing his faint smile and realising she was beginning to jabber. 'How did you know where to find me?' she asked instead.

Broad shoulders lifted in an easy shrug. 'I saw you heading in this direction and took a guess that you'd be staff rather than a customer at that hour. I've been wandering the store for the last fifteen minutes looking for you.'

'Supposing I'd been in the offices?' she suggested, intrigued despite herself.

He laughed. 'That might have fazed me. Anyway, you weren't.'

'No.' Adria scarcely knew what else to say. To the best of her knowledge, she had never seen this man before, yet there was something about him that bothered her. Around thirty-three or four, she guessed, some six feet or more in height, and well built under the tailored grey suit that almost matched the colour of his eyes. A man of some means, there was little doubt about that. There was an air of authority, even a touch of arrogance in the set of the dark head. His mouth drew her eyes: firmly moulded, tilted now at the corners in that slow smile, it both fascinated and strangely repelled. Sensual, came the fleeting thought, sending a sudden tiny tremor along her spine. 'Look, I'm really sorry if I gave you a shock this morning,' she added haltingly. 'If the car had caught me it would have been my fault, not yours. What else . . .'

'I didn't come looking for you to extract an apology,' he denied. 'But if you feel you owe me one, I'll settle for dinner tonight.'

Green eyes darkened. 'Thanks, I don't think so.'

'Meaning you don't go out with total strangers?' The smile was still there, still not reaching the eyes that watched and weighed and veiled the thoughts behind them. 'That's a matter easily rectified. I'm Kyle Hamilton, from St Amelia.'

Her brow creased a little. 'St Amelia?'

'It's an island in the Caribbean. One of the Virgin group.' There was a kind of deliberation in the way he pronounced the words. 'We produce rum.'

'That's fascinating.' She was relieved to see a young woman pause at one of the displays further along the counter. 'I'm sorry, you'll have to excuse me. I have a customer.'

If she had hoped he might take the hint she was to be disappointed. He was standing in the same spot, looking anything but patient, when she finally completed the sale.

'You didn't tell me your name,' he said, as if there had been no interruption in the conversation.

'I know.' She gave him a straight glance. 'I didn't think it was necessary. Thank you for the invitation, Mr Hamilton, but I'm afraid I already have an engagement this evening.'

'I see.' The shrug came again, lightly resigned. 'In that case, I'll be getting along. Take care.'

Adria watched him walk away, her teeth catching at her lower lip. She had wanted him to go, yet now that he had, she regretted her abruptness. Would it really have done any harm to be pleasant to the man? Whatever his motives, he had at least taken the trouble to find her. For that effort alone he deserved commendation. He attracted her, she was bound to acknowledge that much. He had the kind of forceful personality many women were drawn to. She had no engagement for this evening, and no doubt they would not have been dining at any second-rate venue.

Too late now, anyway. He had disappeared. Probably as well, considering. He was just another tourist, here on a fleeting visit and looking for some casual companionship. It was doubtful if he would be without for long.

'You're looking pensive,' remarked her fellow assistant, whom she hadn't noticed approaching. 'Feeling all right?'

Adria summoned a smile and a nod. 'Just thinking. I started the stock-check while you were upstairs.'

'I'll get on with it, then, while you take your break,' acknowledged the other cheerfully. 'If you'll take some advice, you'll plump for tea this morning. I think somebody left a dishcloth in the coffee-pot!'

It was a long day, made longer by the lightness of trade. Obviously the tourists preferred to be outside taking advantage of the heatwave conditions to see the sights of London. The moment the weather broke they would come flocking back. Adria only hoped it would at least last through the following afternoon. She planned to spend it at the local Lido, sunbathing.

The sun was still giving out considerable heat when she left the store at five-thirty. She paused just outside the staff entrance doorway to adjust the strap of her high-heeled sandal, holding on to the stonework with one hand for support.

'Need any help?' asked a male voice from behind her, and she straightened abruptly to look up into familiar grey eyes with that same odd sensation deep down inside her.

'It isn't broken,' she denied. 'Just slipping. I've tightened it, so it should be OK now.'

'Good. Wouldn't do to fall and break an ankle.' He studied her quizzically. 'Surprised to see me again?'

'Frankly, yes,' she admitted.

'You thought I'd accepted the brush-off?' He shook his head, mouth tilting. 'Opposition only serves to whet the appetite for battle, didn't you know that?'

'Meaning you're not accustomed to being turned down?'

He laughed. 'That might have some bearing. Anyway, nothing ventured, nothing gained. I've been waiting out here since just gone five so as to be sure not to miss you.'

Her gaze was direct. 'Why?'

'Because I'd still like to take you out to dinner.'

'I told you . . .' she began.

'I know what you told me,' he interrupted smoothly. 'I think that was just an excuse.'

'You think it so unlikely I might already have a date?'

'No,' he said, 'it just came out a little too pat, that's all. Still, I could have been wrong. *Do* you have a date?'

Adria hesitated before slowly shaking her head, urged by some emotion not easy to define. 'An excuse, like you said.'

The smile widened briefly. 'Well, I'm nothing if not persistent. Have dinner with me. We can have a drink somewhere first.'

Her protest was rhetorical; she knew it and she knew he knew it too. 'I'm not dressed for going out.'

He slid a glance over her slender figure outlined by the classically-styled cream linen dress, coming back to linger for a moment on the smooth fall of chestnut hair. 'You look perfect. Good enough for the Ritz!'

It was Adria's turn to laugh. 'I'd as soon go somewhere less imposing.'

'Whatever you like.' He took the question as settled, placing a light touch under her elbow to indicate the direction he wanted her to go. 'I left the car round the corner on double yellow lines. It will be a miracle if I don't have a ticket by now.'

Miracles, it appeared, were not in the offing. Kyle pulled a wry face as he slid the paper from beneath his wiper blade before coming to join Adria in the car.

'The third today,' he confessed, tossing the ticket into the glove compartment to join those already there. 'Suppose I should have listened to advice and used taxis, only I hate being driven. I'm staying at Claridge's. We'll drop down there for a drink and leave the car for the evening. Make things easier.'

Drinks at Claridge's, thought Adria with humour; she was going up in the world! 'Shall you plead guilty?' she asked lightly. 'To the parking offences, I mean.'

'I'll be leaving the country come the weekend,' he returned, equally lightly, starting the engine, 'so the question isn't likely to arise. Not unless they want to chase me out to the Caribbean.'

The sunlight seemed to have dimmed a little. Adria stole a glance at the lean profile as they pulled away from the kerb, registering the clean line of jaw and throat, the crisp thickness of his hair. He had the seat set well back to allow room for long legs, thigh muscles tensing beneath the fine material as he depressed the clutch for a gear change. His hands on the wheel were long-fingered and fleshless, the sinews clearly visible beneath the skin. He wore a gold signet ring on the near little finger, its only decoration an interwoven KH. A pulse throbbed suddenly at the base of her throat. She swallowed hard, feeling pressure in her ears the same way one felt it when making a descent in a plane. Except she had never been in a plane—not to her knowledge.

Kyle seemed to sense some change in the atmosphere, eyes briefly flicking her way. 'Feeling all right?'

'Yes.' She struggled to regain her equilibrium. 'Yes, fine. Is this your own car?'

'Hired.' From the note in his voice, he was as fully aware of the superfluity of the question as she was herself. 'Naturally, I'll make sure the rental company aren't going to be out of pocket when it comes to paying any fines.'

It wasn't why she had said it, but she let it ride. Her head felt as if it were stuffed with cotton wool. That ring—or one like it—meant something to her, she was almost certain. She could still see it in front of her eyes, the gold glinting as if caught by sunlight. Then the image was gone, her head clearing, the sounds around her returning to normal. It had happened before like this, but never for as long. If only she could break through the fog at the back of her mind!

She was outwardly in control of herself by the time they reached the hotel, although her legs still felt a bit wobbly when she stood. Kyle handed over the car keys to the doorman, who obviously knew him, and took Adria through to the bar.

'You'd better have a brandy,' he stated when they were seated at a table, eyeing her judiciously. 'I thought you were going to pass out on me in the car.'

'Nothing serious,' she said on a casual note. 'I'm perfectly all right now.' She conjured a smile. 'Anyway, I can't stand brandy. Make it a gin and tonic instead, will you, please?'

'You know best.' He ordered whisky for himself from the waiter who appeared at his elbow, then sat back in his seat to say levelly, 'I still don't know your name.'

There was no hesitation, because it was the only name by which she knew herself. 'Adria Morris.'

'Adria? That's unusual.'

'One of the reasons . . .' She caught herself up, feeling the blood come up in her face and then recede. One of the reasons I chose it, she had been about to say, which was true enough. She had wanted something different, something that gave her individuality. The Morris had been picked out with a pin. 'One of the reasons my parents chose it,' she substituted, turning the pause into a cough. 'Excuse me, I've got a tickle in my throat.'

Although he made no comment, she was fairly sure he had noted her momentary confusion. The arrival of their drinks created a welcome diversion. By the time they were settled again she was able to meet the grey eyes without a flicker. 'You said this morning you lived on an island. Is it very large?'

'A few square miles,' he acknowledged.

'Who owns it?'

Kyle smiled and lifted his shoulders. 'As the only surviving male of the family, I suppose you'd have to say I do. My brother died a couple of years ago. He was killed in a car accident.'

'I'm sorry.' It sounded lame, yet there was little else one could say. 'Do you have any sisters?'

'One. And my mother is still alive. They both live with me.'

'And you make rum?'

'That's right. We have our own distillery. Did you ever visit the Caribbean?'

Adria shook her head. It was a fairly safe bet, she told herself.

'You should. There's no place better. Few ups and downs in weather conditions, for one thing. The beaches around St Amelia are second to none.'

He would look good in trunks, came the fleeting thought; long, strong limbs deeply tanned, chest broad, well-muscled, covered in tight whorls of hair. She blinked, astonished by the vividness of the image. It was going a bit far. She had only just met the man!

'Sounds wonderful!' she agreed, forcing a casual note. 'You're fortunate to live in such a lovely part of the world.'

'There have been Hamiltons on the island for almost three hundred years,' he acknowledged. 'I couldn't live anywhere else.'

'But if you're the last of the line ...'

His smile was slightly cynical. 'If I fail to marry and produce a son then it will be up to my sister to persuade the man she marries to change his name to Hamilton by deed poll.'

He wasn't married. Her mind seized on the information. Not that it really made very much difference. After this evening she would most likely never see Kyle Hamilton again.

'Anyway,' he was saying now, 'that's enough about me. Tell me about yourself?'

She looked down at her glass. 'There's very little to tell.' She could say that much with truth, at any rate, as far as it went. 'I live in a bedsit right here in London, and you already know what I do as a job.'

'No family?'

'None that I know of.' Green eyes met and held grey without flinching. 'I'm used to it.'

'I wasn't about to start breaking out in sympathy,' Kyle denied with an edge of irony. 'You're obviously quite self-contained. However, point taken. You'd rather not talk about it.'

She said swiftly. 'I just don't happen to consider there's anything worth talking about, that's all.' She laughed, trying for a lighter note. 'If I find it boring, it stands to reason other people are going to.'

'Not necessarily, but we won't argue about it.' He paused, eyes reflective as they scanned her face. 'Do you like Italian food?'

It took her a moment to adjust. 'Why—yes.'

'Right. I'd better make sure they have a table for us first.' He was getting to his feet as he spoke. 'Just a phone call. It won't take long.'

She didn't turn her head to watch him as he left the bar.

A part of her mind was telling her urgently to leave now while she had the chance, while another part wanted as desperately to stay. Kyle Hamilton was not going to be a man easily forgotten, that much she already knew. He aroused emotions in her not yet fully defined. In some ways she was almost afraid of him. When he turned that steely grey gaze on her he seemed to see through to her very soul.

He was back before she had come to any firm decision. ' All fixed,' he declared, taking his seat again. 'Seven-thirty all right for you?'

'Fine,' said Adria, 'but I'd have thought . . .'

'Thought what?' Kyle prompted as she broke off, and she laughed a little self-consciously.

'Oh, just a notion that you'd be more accustomed to eating late, coming from the tropics.'

'Sub-tropics,' he corrected lightly. 'And there's no hard and fast rule. The time to eat is when you're hungry. I've been out and around all day.'

She lifted her glass and drank from it, more for something to do than through any real desire for alcohol. 'You've been back to the hotel before this, though.'

'How did you know that?'

'You're wearing a different shirt, for one thing, and you've shaved again since this morning—at least, it looks like it.'

One hand went up to smooth his jaw-line, his smile dry. 'Top marks for observation. There's nothing worse than five o'clock shadow when you're trying to impress a woman!'

'Are you?' she asked without meaning to. 'Trying to impress me, I mean.'

'What do you think?' His voice was lacking in any kind of mockery. 'I can hardly be the first. You're a very lovely girl, Adria.'

'I was a woman a moment ago,' she pointed out, trying to retain a steady head. 'Why the sudden demotion?'

The amusement kindling his gaze was genuine. 'I can see I'm going to have to watch my step with you. How old are you, anyway?'

'As old as my tongue and a little bit older than my . . .' She pulled herself up, shaking her head in self-deprecation. 'Sorry about that. It's a stupid saying. I'm twenty-four.'

'About what I thought. Gives me a ten-year advantage. Do you think it's too much?'

'Considering you'll be on your way back to St Amelia come the weekend, I think it's immaterial,' she responded in the same vein. 'I could add something about ships that pass in the night, but I won't.'

'Thank heaven for that small mercy!' He was laughing with her, looking suddenly younger, carefree—catching at her heartstrings in a way she found difficult to conceal. Her fingers ached to reach out and touch those firm lips, to trace their shape. She wanted to say his name. Kyle. So strong and masculine. Men like him were all too rare.

That was an opinion she was to underline during the rest of the evening. Enjoying the superb meal, chatting about this and that, sharing the odd joke, she felt herself becoming more and more enmeshed. When they danced together she melted in his arms, not thinking of anything much beyond the sensations created by his closeness. His breath was warm against her temple, his hands supportive at her back, holding her secure—safe. Safe from what, she didn't stop to ask herself. It was enough that he was there.

'You gave me a shock in more ways than one this morning,' he admitted at one point when they were sitting out a session. 'You're very nearly the double of someone I once knew.' He registered her swift change of expression with a faint smile. 'They say we all have a *doppelgänger* somewhere in the world.'

'Am I like her in any other ways?' Adria heard herself ask.

Something in him seemed to harden for a moment, then he smiled again and the moment was past. 'Not really. Just a coincidental arrangement of features, that's all.' There was a pause, a change of tone. 'Are we going to do this again before I leave?'

She could feel her heart thudding against her ribs, the mingling of gladness and sadness inside her. Two more days, three at the most, and he would be gone. It was unlikely that they would ever meet again. More sensible, surely, to finish it now before she fell any further? 'If you want to,' she said.

'I'd hardly be asking otherwise. I could pick you up again from work tomorrow.'

'It's my half day.'

'Better still. We can run down to Brighton and get some sea air before we dine. I'll get a picnic lunch fixed up. What say you?'

'It sounds nice.' Nice! Such a trite word to describe the delicious anticipation singing through her veins. So she was heading for a badly bent, if not exactly broken, heart. Pleasure had to be paid for in one measure or another.

She was half relieved, half disappointed when Kyle made no attempt to see her all the way home. He put her into a taxi outside the restaurant and paid the driver before coming back to the open rear window to say succinctly, 'Twelve-thirty.'

Thirteen hours, she thought as the vehicle pulled away from the kerb. Unlucky for some, perhaps, but not for her. In thirteen hours she would be with Kyle again, a whole half day stretching before them. Odd to think that only this morning she hadn't even known of his existence. He hadn't kissed her goodnight, although she had expected it. His whole attitude was so different from what she might have expected, considering the circumstances of their relationship. Perhaps he himself preferred to shy clear of any physical involvement on such a short-term basis.

It was almost midnight when the taxi dropped her outside the shabby Victorian house she called home. Most windows were still lit, the sounds from a couple of tape decks clearly audible even out here in the street. Adria knew her fellow lodgers only slightly; she rarely saw anyone else. Her immediate neighbour on the landing was a man in his forties who was so shy he went blood-red if she so much as said good morning when they happened to meet on the stairs. His history couldn't be very happy either, she always imagined.

Scantily furnished, her own room was one of the smaller ones. Adria had made it as pleasant as she could with the use of paint and paper, and some bright curtains and cushions. A screen painted to match the wall colour cut off the sink and small stove in the far corner. That too was her own idea. It gave some illusion of separate facilities. There were two bathrooms between seven people, which was a whole lot better than some premises she and Larry had viewed. Nevertheless, it was getting towards the point where she needed to move on. With last month's rise taken into account, she could afford something a little more up-market—always providing it could be found, of course.

Lying in the narrow divan later, she found sleep difficult to come by. Kyle's face kept getting in the way. He was older than Larry by six years, but it wasn't only age that made the differences so apparent. Kyle moved in another world, lived a lifestyle far removed from any with which Larry might come into contact. The former wouldn't know what it was to worry about where the next month's rent was coming from, or to face the possibility of having essential services cut off due to non-payment of bills. He had probably never had to worry about a thing in his whole life. Of the two of them, Larry was perhaps the more worthy character, yet she had to acknowledge the fact that he didn't attract her in quite the same way Kyle did. Her pulses still sang from that encounter.

She slept at last, to dream of sun-washed beaches and white sands, of splashing through warm shallows with laughter on her lips and a shadowy figure at her side. Not Kyle, she reflected on waking; someone else. Had it been a dream, or a memory dredged up from the past? There was no way of telling.

He was waiting when she left the store on the half-hour. Today he wore pale beige slacks and a toning jacket, his shirt open at the throat on a triangle of dark hair.

'I stuck a tie in the glove compartment for later,' he explained, noting her glance. 'It's too warm for formality right now.'

'I was just thinking how suited to the weather you looked,' Adria denied, playing down her responses. 'This must be more like you're used to at home.'

'Getting on that way.' The eyes appraising her own choice of slim-skirted dress and matching jacket held definite approval. 'Green is a good colour on you. Hope you're good and hungry. I had the hotel make up a hamper.'

Adria laughed. 'I couldn't eat a horse, but I might manage a small pony!'

One of the other girls from her department came out from the store, giving the two of them a speculative glance. Tomorrow there would probably be some comment, but she didn't really care. Here and now was all that mattered. It was the happiest she had felt in the whole two years of her remembered existence. No, not just happy, she corrected herself—alive!

This time, Kyle had managed to find a meter. By one o'clock they were clear of the inner-city traffic and heading out to open country. He drove with the air-conditioning turned off and all four windows down for free passage of fresh air through the car. Adria fancied he would use an open-top back home—always providing they used motorised transport on the island at all. From the colour of his skin, she could tell that he spent as little time as possible indoors. She envied him that freedom of choice, if nothing else.

When they finally stopped to eat lunch it was well off the beaten track down a shady lane that ended in open fields and a superb view. Kyle drew the car under a tree to keep the sun off it, while Adria busied herself laying out the contents of the hamper on the chequered cloth provided. There was even a bottle of champagne in its own chiller to go with the roast chicken salad and sundry other items— plus a couple of glasses from which to drink it.

'One each,' said Kyle, pouring for them both. 'If I'm going to be bound by the drink-drive laws then so are you!'

'You don't intend getting me drunk so you can have your way with me, then?' suggested Adria lightly, and felt her colour come up as his expression underwent a sudden change. 'Sorry, that was a ridiculous thing to say,' she apologised. 'It was meant as a joke.'

'Not so ridiculous.' His voice sounded odd, and the grey eyes narrowed slightly as they studied her. 'It might even have been in my mind when I ordered the champagne in the first place.'

'Now *you're* joking!' She tried to laugh the moment off. 'I don't imagine you'd ever find need to stoop to subterfuge.'

'Depends on circumstances.' The smile was back,

curving his lips with a slowness that tautened her stomach muscles. 'I don't deny I'd like to make love to you, Adria. You have all the attributes to get a man thinking along those lines from the word go. On the other hand, you don't come across as the type likely to give it away to all and sundry just for the asking.'

'And you're hardly going to be in the country long enough to change my mind,' she agreed, borrowing his tone. 'Nice to have that settled, anyway.'

'I could always extend my stay.' The offer was softly made. 'Would you be willing to keep me company if I did?'

She stared at him, not entirely sure if he was serious. Her heartbeats were faster, almost as if she had been running. 'I might consider it,' she managed at last, with creditable composure.

'Then it's definitely worth thinking about.' He had left his jacket in the car, turning back his sleeves over muscular forearms. Unexpectedly, he stretched out a hand and ran the back of his knuckles gently down her cheek, registering the darkening of her eyes with a narrowing of his own. She was still holding the glass when he kissed her. Sparkling liquid splashed on to her bare skin as it tilted, but she scarcely noticed the dampness. His lips were firm and compelling, cool on the surface yet so warm in intent. She felt the glass taken from her hand, his weight pressing her back into the grass, the thickness of his hair beneath her fingers. Larry had kissed her on occasion, only never like this. There was a buzzing in her ears, a dizziness in her mind, a sense of falling as if the world itself was turning upside down.

The touch of his hand at her breast aroused no protest from her. It seemed so natural that he should caress her this way. There was the coolness of air on her heated flesh as he drew away the covering material, the tingling intimacy of his fingers exploring the firm curve, the tender torment when he brushed her hardened nipple, followed by a sharply indrawn breath as he bent his head to follow the same path with his mouth.

She wanted this man, there was no doubting that fact now. The need was swamping her. The sudden, abrupt lift of his head was a deprivation. When she opened her eyes he was staring down at her exposed skin, the expression in his eyes one of utter incredulity.

'It's only a birthmark,' she murmured, guessing what was drawing his attention if not entirely understanding the strength of his reaction. 'A little crescent moon.'

'I know what it is.' His voice was frightening in its harshness. He sat up straight, dragging her with him, his fingers digging into the bones of her shoulders, face a hard mask. 'Just what game is it you've been playing, Lisa?'

CHAPTER TWO

THE buzzing in her ears had increased, drowning out rational thought. She could only stare at him, eyes wide and dark in the sudden sickly pallor of her face.

'Answer me, damn you!' he gritted.

'I don't know what you're talking about.' Her voice seemed to be coming from a long way off. 'Who is Lisa?'

'Stop the play-acting!' He shook her, jaw clenched so hard the bone jutted at each point. 'I don't know how or why, but I know who! There can't be two of you with the same features and colouring *and* a birthmark in the same place. That's stretching coincidence just too far!'

'I'm sorry.' She was trembling, nausea rising inside her, her whole mind reeling in shock. Then she went cold, very cold, and everything dimmed.

She was lying flat on her back when she came round again. Kyle knelt over her, blocking out the sun, his eyes full of concern. He held her wrist between finger and thumb, registering the uneven pulsebeat. An exclamation of relief escaped his lips as she opened her eyes.

'Thank God,' he said. 'I thought you were dead for a minute back there! I couldn't find any pulse. No, don't move. You still look like death.'

'I'm sorry,' she said again, obeying the injunction for the simple reason that her limbs felt too weak and shaky to prop her up. 'I just . . . I can't . . .'

'No, *I'm* sorry.' He sounded it, too. 'You couldn't have acted these last few minutes. No one could.' The grey eyes studied her, perplexed, uncertain. 'I feel pretty shaken up myself. If you're really Adria Morris, that means . . .'

25

'I'm not.' It was no more than a whisper. 'I don't know who I am. I haven't known for more than two years.'

'Two years?' The perplexity was still there but altered in character. 'What . . .'

'I don't have any memory of before that. Adria Morris was a name I chose myself because I had to be called something.' She searched the lean features, looking for she knew not what. 'Who is this . . . Lisa?'

'My sister-in-law.' He said it as if the words were dragged from him. 'My brother's wife.'

Her throat contracted. 'The one who was killed?'

'Yes.' Kyle sat back slowly, pushing a distracted hand through his hair. He was pale himself under the tan, face drawn. 'Except that she was killed with him. We buried the two of them in the family crypt back there on St Amelia.' He turned his head to look at her again. 'You're no ghost, that's for sure! It's about the only thing that is.'

Adria pushed herself upright. She felt trembly and weak, but at least her limbs would obey her. She made a valiant attempt to bring her mind under the same control. As Kyle had said a moment or two ago, coincidence could be stretched just so far. There had to be some logical explanation—some tying together of the two factors, no matter how unlikely. If she wasn't Adria Morris then she could only be Lisa Hamilton. Except that Lisa Hamilton was dead. Killed in a car crash, from what Kyle had intimated. How could she be a dead woman?

'Did you actually see the body?' she heard herself asking.

'No.' A muscle jerked at the side of his mouth. 'The car caught fire. They were both of them too badly burned for visual indentification. Difficult to believe there could be any mistake. They were seen together in the car only an hour or so before the crash. She . . .' He stopped there, shaking his head with an air of confusion. 'You'd better fill me in on your story,' he added. 'It might help.'

It took her only a few minutes, and provided little help at all. 'Victoria,' he mused. 'I suppose it's just barely possible you could have come in from Heathrow. They didn't leave you anything?'

'Only the clothes I stood up in.' Adria had an arm wrapped about her knees, hugging herself for warmth, although the sun still beat down.

'Do you still have them?'

'Yes.' Her smile felt cracked. 'That dress was my only connection with the past. I haven't worn it since, but I couldn't bring myself to get rid of it either. It's hanging in the wardrobe back in my room.'

'Right.' Kyle got to his feet, looking down at her with an air of purpose. 'Feel well enough to travel?'

'Of course.' She took his extended hand, resisting the desire to hold on to it for support when she was standing again. 'We're going back to town?'

'I want to see that dress,' he acknowledged. 'I might be able to recognise it.'

Green eyes met grey. 'And if you don't?'

'We'll cover that if and when we come to it. Go and sit in the car while I get this lot packed up. You still look pretty shaky.'

She still felt it. Sitting in the front passenger seat, she closed her eyes and tried to bring some order to chaos. The whole thing was fantastic, yet it could hardly be dismissed. Lisa Hamilton. The first name meant nothing to her, the second was familiar only because she had already heard it in connection with Kyle. If she really did turn out to be his sister-in-law then it opened up a bewildering number of questions. They had buried two people out there in the Caribbean, one of them, it could be assumed, female. If not Lisa—who? And how could Lisa herself have been in London when she had been seen with her husband only an hour before the crash? Adria put up both hands to press her temples, feeling her head would burst from the strain.

'Try not to let it get to you,' Kyle advised, slinging the hamper on the rear seat. 'All we're doing at the moment is going around in circles.' He came to slide behind the wheel, closing the door and switching on the ignition in one smooth movement. 'The dress first, then we'll take it from there.'

They neither of them spoke very much on the way. Adria stared out of the window, seeing nothing of the passing scene. The happiness she had felt earlier was past and gone; she felt heavy, listless, head aching. Whatever the truth, she was no closer to remembering. Beyond that same two-year gap her mind remained blank as ever.

The house appeared deserted when they reached it. Letting herself in with the front-door key, Adria led the way upstairs to her first-floor room. With Kyle in it, the room seemed even more restricted than usual. He made no comment but she felt the disdain in his swift appraisal. Not what he was used to, that was for sure. Not what his brother's wife would have been used to, either.

She went over to the wardrobe to find the dress, closing her fingers over the hanger with a sense of fatalism, as if everything hinged on this moment. When she turned, Kyle was standing close behind her.

'Hold it up against you,' he said.

Adria did so, watching his face for some sign of recognition. The slow shake of his head was a hammer blow to any hope she might have had in her heart.

'Would you necessarily have known every garment she had in her wardrobe?' she asked on a note of desperation.

'No,' he admitted. 'It was a long shot, I agree, but it had to be tried.'

She turned a little to view the dress herself in the long mirror attached to the inner door of the wardrobe, fingering the satiny smoothness of the cotton. 'It's better quality than any I could afford now,' she murmured, almost to herself. 'Does *Honore* mean anything to you?'

Kyle was still within view through the mirror. His eyes had narrowed. 'Say again?'

'*Honore*. It's the name on the dress label. They tried to trace it but couldn't.'

'Let me see.' He was right behind her, taking the garment from her to turn back the collar. For a moment he was quite still, expression difficult to read, then he glanced up again at her and there was reconciliation in his eyes. '*Honore* is the designer name of an exclusive boutique in Charlotte Amalie.'

'That's the capital of St Thomas, isn't it?'

'Yes, it is.' The pause was brief but weighted. 'The crash happened on St Thomas, shortly after you and Paul got there.' He searched her face, looking for some sign. 'Nothing?'

Slowly she shook her head. Paul. It was the first time Kyle had mentioned his brother's name. His brother, her husband. No, it just wasn't possible! How could any woman forget the man she had married—or even that she *was* married? Yet the probability had been there right from the start, hadn't it? No ring, just a paler gap on the third finger of her left hand. Her skin tone had excited no particular interest. It had been an exceptional spring that year. There had been some suggestion of trauma brought on by the break-up of a relationship, but enquiries had failed to take that theory any further, either.

'I feel so odd,' she whispered.

'Then you'd better sit down.'

There was no point in telling him it was a mental rather than a physical strangeness. For two years she had been living in limbo; now she had a background again. It had to be true. There was no other feasible explanation.

'Tell me about her,' she begged as he put her into the

room's only chair. 'There might be something . . .'

Kyle took a seat on the edge of the divan, resting his elbows on his knees and running a hand around the back of his neck as though to ease an ache. 'I'm not sure how to start. The day Paul brought you back with him to St Amelia was the first any of us had heard of you. He met you on a skiing holiday in Switzerland. You were married there.'

'He just turned up out of the blue with a wife?' She could scarcely believe that either. 'What kind of man would do a thing like that?'

'Paul was far from predictable.' The tone held irony. 'He acted on impulse rather than reason. He saw you, he wanted you, so he married you—at least, that's the way he told it.'

'How long ago?'

'Less than three months before the accident. It made things even more tragic in the eyes of those who didn't know the true facts.'

Her eyes were fastened on the lean face. 'Which were?'

'That you were washed up anyway.'

His voice had hardened. Adria felt herself change colour; go hot and then cold. 'Did you know the reason?'

'The main reason was you were never suited in the first place. You . . .' He broke off, shaking his head as if to dismiss what he had been about to say. 'It's immaterial now. What we need to find out is how you landed up here in England.'

'And who the other woman was,' she said with deliberation.

'Other woman?'

'The one you buried in my place—always providing I really am Lisa.'

'If there was any doubt at all, there's none now. That dress label proves it.'

She was bound to agree with that assessment. One coincidence perhaps, maybe even two at a pinch, but they were being bombarded with them. Lisa Hamilton. It still meant nothing to her. She had no picture of Paul in her mind, only of this man seated before her.

'It might be immaterial to you,' she got out, 'but I need to know everything. What about before I met your brother?'

'Your maiden name was Cosgrove. According to what you told us, you were orphaned at an early age and brought up by an aunt who was your only remaining family. When she died she left you some money.'

'Enough to take me to Switzerland?'

'Apparently. By the way,' he added on the same unemotional note, 'you're twenty-three, not four. You had your twenty-first birthday in the April.'

'What date?'

'The fourteenth.' He met her seeking gaze with a shrug. 'That's about the whole of it. You were never very forthcoming about your background.'

'It seems I didn't have much of a one to talk about.' She was hanging on to her balance by a thread. 'You didn't approve of the marriage, that goes without saying. How about the rest of the family?'

'My mother wasn't over-enthusiastic. She had great hopes for her younger son.' His tone was dry. 'Madalyn?' Again the shrug. 'She's a law unto herself.'

'Meaning she refused to condemn me out of hand as a gold-digger?' The retort was sharp. 'That's what you're intimating, isn't it? That I trapped your brother into marrying me because I wanted a rich husband!'

'For someone with no memory you come pretty close to the mark,' he responded coolly. 'It was one theory, yes. He told me you refused to sleep with him before you were married.'

Her colour rose again. 'How many men would marry a

girl just because he couldn't have her any other way?'

'Paul might have. What he wanted he had to have—any way he could.'

She said softly, 'I don't think you liked him very much, if the truth were known.'

'We were different,' he said, unmoved by the suggestion. 'The seven years between us didn't help. And is all this really getting us anywhere?'

'Not so far,' she was bound to admit. 'There isn't even a spark.'

Kyle was silent for a long moment, face unrevealing. 'Has there been?' he asked at length. 'Anything at all? You looked quite thrown yesterday when I turned up at your counter in the shop.'

'Only because I recognised you as the man who'd almost run me down.' She rose abruptly to her feet, going to the window to stand looking out on to the narrow street. 'To be honest, I'm not all that sure I even want to remember any more.'

'Because you don't like what you've heard?'

'Your version of it, no.'

'But if you can't remember, you can't be sure I was wrong.'

She spun round on him, eyes suddenly blazing. 'Don't you think I realise that? How do you think it feels to have no memory? You can look back over thirty-odd years, I've got two. You know yourself, I only know the person I've had to become. There's one thing I am sure of, though, and that's that basic character doesn't alter. If I couldn't think of marrying a man for his money now, I couldn't have done it then either!'

Kyle said softly, 'You're saying you really loved him?'

'Oh, God I don't know!' She made a helpless gesture with her hands. 'I must have done.'

'So we'll let it ride at that. The important thing is where

we go from here.' There was a lengthy pause. When he spoke again it was on a constrained note, as if something within him battled against the actual words. 'You realise you're heir to half the estate?'

She gaped at him, heart thudding painfully against her rib-cage. 'What are you talking about?'

'Exactly what I say. As Paul's widow you're entitled to all his worldly goods. The Hamilton estate normally descends through the male line in order of seniority, but I made Paul a full partner.' His expression was controlled. 'It's yours now, along with everything else he left.'

'I don't want it!' The denial was jerked from her. 'It doesn't have anything to do with me!'

'You're his widow. Regardless of the whys and where-fores, that's still a fact.' The grey eyes were almost clinical in their assessment. 'You have to come back to St Amelia, Lisa. It's the only place to start sorting things out.'

Lisa, Lisa—that wasn't her name! But then neither was Adria. She was a non-person; she always would be a non-person unless she recovered her memory. If she could do that anywhere it would be St Amelia. Something had happened to Lisa out there, something that had sent her running back to England. What Kyle was offering her now was the chance to become whole again. Could she afford to turn her back on it?

He was watching her, registering the emotions chasing across her face. When he spoke again his voice had softened a fraction. 'There's no doubt in my mind. Not any more. When I first saw you darting across that road I thought I was imagining the likeness. I came looking for you because curiosity alone wouldn't let me do anything else. You're different, Lisa, but not different enough. There were moments last night when I felt ...' He paused, jaw-line tensing as if he had been about to say something he shouldn't. 'It's not important now. I'm convinced. You have to be, too. How else could you have come by that dress?'

'I know. I believe you.' The tremor was still there in her voice. 'I'm just not sure I can leave everything I've built up over the last two years here.'

'Such as what?' With a disparaging glance around the room. 'You can hardly call this place home—or your job a career.' He paused again, his gaze sharpening a fraction. 'Unless there's some other reason for staying. A man, perhaps?'

She shook her head. 'Nothing serious, or I wouldn't have accepted your invitation last night.'

'So what's to stop you?'

'You, for one thing.' She could no longer contain the accusation. 'Your whole attitude towards me has changed since you found out who I might be.'

'Who you are,' he corrected. 'I thought we agreed there's no might about it. And of course I've changed. You're my brother's widow. For two years I've believed you dead. Don't you think that calls for some mental adjustment on my part, too?'

There was more to it than that, and they both knew it, she thought. Kyle hadn't trusted his sister-in-law. If she had given him good cause, then she wasn't the kind of person she took herself to be now. Yet could she allow that possibility to put her off? Wasn't the need to discover her past more pressing than the fear of what she might find? She had to go back. There was no other choice. If she couldn't recover the past she could perhaps redress it.

She took a good deep breath before saying it, conscious of burning all her boats behind her. 'All right, I'll come to St Amelia.'

The grey eyes were unfathomable. 'I'll phone through with the news. How long will you need?'

'I hadn't thought that far ahead,' she confessed. 'I'll have to ask for leave of absence from work, and then there's this place. The rent is paid for the coming month, so ...'

'If you come back at all,' he pointed out, 'it will be as a very rich young woman. You won't need a job, and you certainly won't need *this* place. Tell them the truth at the store. I'm sure they'll appreciate the position.'

'I can't do it in less than a week,' she insisted. 'Why don't you go ahead and I'll follow?'

His mouth firmed. 'I'll wait. You need someone around to keep reminding you who you are.'

There was some truth in that, she was bound to acknowledge. Even now, her mind kept repudiating the evidence. She was Lisa Hamilton; not only must she keep telling herself that, but she must learn to think it, too. Adria Morris no longer existed.

It was raining when the plane for New York lifted off. Watching the drenched landscape slip away beneath the wings, Lisa wondered how long it would be before she saw it again. The past week had been fraught, to say the least. She had given in her notice without stating her reasons, preferring they should take it she had another job to go to. Word had got round, of course, but those who had taken the trouble to ask were little the wiser for the exercise. There had been no collection for a leaving present, nor would she have expected one. She had never been on that sort of footing with her fellow employees.

Larry was the only one to whom she had told the truth of the matter; news he had received with obvious mixed feelings. While in little doubt that she should grasp at any chance of recovering her memory, he foresaw difficulties ahead in her relationship with the Hamiltons. Kyle himself he regarded with certain reservations—probably, as he was ready to admit, because the other man was his antithesis in almost every way.

'Look after her,' he had admonished at the airport, where he had insisted on coming to see them off. 'She's already been through one bad experience.'

'You know he's in love with you,' Kyle had said quietly as they moved on into passport control.

'No, he isn't,' she had told him with conviction. 'Larry's in love with his work.'

Thinking about it now, she saw no reason to change that opinion. She and Larry had been good friends, nothing more. Oh, they had kissed from time to time, true, but he had never shown any real inclination to move on from there—nor would she have wanted him to. She had promised to keep in touch, and she would. It was always nice to know there was someone she could turn back to if the going became too rough.

It had proved possible to obtain a copy of her original birth certificate in the name of Lisa Cosgrove. The names given as those of the parents had meant nothing to her, and an attempt to contact someone at the address stated had proved fruitless. With a copy of the marriage certificate wired post-haste from Fribourg, they had been able to secure a passport made out to Mrs Lisa Hamilton and obtain a US visa. Seeing it down there in black and white had given her no sense of belonging. She might call herself by that name, but she was still a nonentity in her own mind. She could only hope that feeling would eventually fade.

They were travelling first class, of course: a habit to which, she thought with an edge of cynicism, she could easily become addicted. Lunch was served on real china instead of the plastic trays which were the norm back in economy, the food itself of superior quality. She had travelled on planes before; she knew that for a fact now. The trip to Switzerland, for instance. Why Switzerland? she asked herself, not for the first time. Had she been a keen skier already, or had she simply considered it the most likely place to find a rich husband? One thing was certain: there was going to be little chance of testing her proficiency on the snow slopes where she was going.

The stewardess brought coffee, leaning across to smile at Lisa. 'Black or white, Mrs Hamilton?'

Mrs Hamilton. Would she ever get used to being called that? It was fairly apparent that the cabin crew took it for granted she and Kyle were married to each other. He hadn't corrected the error, although it wouldn't have passed him by, either. At thirty-four it was past time he began thinking about finding himself a wife—unless he already had someone lined up. Her mind shied away from that thought. Luxury or no luxury, this journey threatened to become tedious. From New York they were to fly down to St Thomas in the US Virgin group where they would spend the night. The following day would see them on yet another plane to Tortola in the British sector, and finally a boat trip to St Amelia. The last time she had taken this same outward route it had been as a bride with her new husband at her side. How would she have felt on that long-ago day? Had she really loved him?

She had to stop asking herself these questions to which there were no answers, she reflected wryly. It was a waste of time and effort. If she was meant to recover her memory then it would happen regardless; if not—well, that remained to be seen.

The man at her side this time round was seemingly engrossed again in the paperback he had bought at the airport. Lisa fancied he was using it as an excuse not to converse with her. He might not be her enemy, but he wasn't exactly her friend, either. A man of integrity, who intended to see the right thing done, that about summed him up. The fact that she would have given several fortunes just to feel the way she had felt for those few brief hours they had spent together before all this had come to light was neither here nor there.

They had an hour at Kennedy between planes. With their ticketing already completed all the way through, there was time for a leisurely drink in the airline's VIP lounge before boarding.

Lisa caught Kyle's eye as she lifted her glass, her smile over-bright. 'This is travelling in style!'

His own smile was dry. 'You'll find tomorrow's flight vastly different. I use the seaplane shuttle.'

'It sounds adventurous.' She didn't care what they talked about, Lisa told herself, providing they did talk. Her nerves were strung like piano wires. 'Is it far from Tortola to St Amelia?'

'Half an hour. We're in the dry season, so it should be a calm enough crossing. You're a good sailor anyway.' His tone was steady. 'I took you out a few times.'

'In what?'

'The *Seajade*. She's a ketch-rigged fifty-footer.'

'Two masts,' Lisa murmured almost to herself.

Grey eyes narrowed a fraction. 'You remember her?'

She shook her head, pulling herself together. 'I must have read it somewhere.' It wasn't wholly the truth; she had had a sudden fleeting vision of sails billowing in the wind. Not necessarily a memory, though. Book or film could have supplied the picture in her mind. She added softly, 'If you took me out in your boat you can't have thought me such a bad lot.'

He opened his mouth to reply, then closed it again, his expression undergoing an abrupt change as his gaze went beyond her to the double doors where another passenger had just entered the lounge. Then he was on his feet, holding out a welcoming hand, the smile on his lips plucking at Lisa's heartstrings. 'Imogen. Good to see you!'

'And you.' The woman in the white Chanel suit kissed him full on the lips, ash-blonde hair swinging back from her face as she tilted her chin to look at him. 'I heard you were expected home tomorrow, so I ditched my plans for the weekend in the hope of catching you. It's been an age since you left!'

'Longer than anticipated,' Kyle agreed. 'Something cropped up.'

'Madalyn told me.' Eyes like twin sapphires turned their attention on Lisa, who was still sitting motionlessly where Kyle had left her. 'Hi, there. How are you?'

'Fine, thanks.' Lisa was at a loss for anything else to say. The newcomer was a shock in more ways than one. Tall and slender in the superbly cut suit, she looked like a model. Her face alone would have launched a thousand ships. That she and Kyle were closer than just good friends was more than apparent. The knowledge brought an ache down deep.

Kyle came to the rescue, expression enigmatic. 'You two never met before. This is Imogen Barrymore, from St Thomas.'

'I'd love to think I could be of some help,' said the other before Lisa could come up with any kind of comment. 'Only I never met Paul either.' Her tone held sympathy. 'It must be awful for you, not remembering anything!'

'There's chance yet.' Kyle had the situation well in hand. 'Come and sit down. Did you want a drink?'

'Is there time?' Imogen glanced at her watch. 'No, I'll wait. They'll be calling the flight any minute.'

'You cut it a bit fine,' he agreed, taking a seat between the two of them.

The American laughed. 'You don't know how much! I only spoke to Madalyn an hour ago. You must spend the night at the house, of course. You should have taken that for granted anyway. You know how the parents would feel if they knew you stayed in a hotel.'

'I expect so.' He was relaxed, easy—more like the man

Lisa had first met. 'All right, you're on. Did Madalyn say anything about having us met at Roadtown?'

'Yes, she's sending the launch to meet the shuttle.'

'Good, then I needn't bother phoning.'

Lisa drained her glass, feeling isolated and forgotten as the two of them talked. She was thankful for the call to the plane. At least it gave her something else to think about. If Imogen had never met Paul she couldn't have known Kyle all that long, yet she appeared almost like one of the family. There was no ring on her finger, so they weren't engaged. Only that didn't necessarily mean there was no under-standing between them either.

The first-class section of the 707 was no more than half-full. Imogen swapped her seat for one immediately across the aisle from the two of them, buckling herself in with the insouciance of the regular traveller.

'A pity Concorde can't make this trip,' she commented as the plane began to taxi out to the runway. 'Think of the saving. You came over on it this morning, I guess?'

'Fully booked,' Kyle replied. 'We had to settle for the regular service.'

'Poor you.' She leaned forward a little in order to see Lisa, who had the window seat. 'You must be exhausted!'

I'm not an invalid! Lisa almost snapped back, but bit her tongue in time. The other woman was trying to be friendly; the least she could do was respond in kind. 'It was more boring than tiring,' she acknowledged, forcing a smile. 'I'd already seen the film.'

'You mean Kyle didn't keep you entertained?' She shook her head at him in mock reproach. 'Not like you, darling.'

His shrug made light of the moment. 'You can't win them all.'

There was nothing to be gained from a denial of any innuendo intended. Lisa made a mental note to watch what she said more carefully from now on. Imogen's solicitation

was all surface: there was no real sympathy in the blue eyes,
just cool calculation.

It was like that the whole journey. Lisa had the feeling
that whenever Imogen was around she would make sure she
held centre court. She found refuge in a pretence of sleep
that eventually drifted into actuality, dreaming strange,
disconnected dreams which merged on waking into a vague
impression of people and voices, and words that made no
sense. It was dark outside the port: below she could see the
lights of a city.

'Five minutes and we'll be down,' said Kyle as she sank
back into her seat again. 'Do you feel rested?'

Lisa nodded, not trusting her voice. She felt tense and
nervous and desperate to be home on familiar ground
again, but there was no point in saying so. These islands
were her starting point on the only way back.

CHAPTER THREE

IMOGEN's home was situated on one of the hills overlooking Charlotte Amalie. As Lisa had anticipated, it proved to be a sumptuous place, set in its own grounds with fine views of the harbour and sea.

Mr and Mrs Barrymore were a couple in their late forties who obviously doted on their only daughter. There was a son too, Lisa gathered during the course of the evening, away at present but also expected back any time. Kyle had been greeted like a long lost son himself, his introduction eliciting expressions of concern. They knew about the accident, of course, Mrs Barrymore had told her, but it had happened more than eighteen months before they met Kyle for the first time.

'St Amelia is so isolated,' she said at one point when they were finishing dinner. 'You must come and stay here with us any time you want to do some shopping, or just for a change.'

'Thank you, I'll remember that,' Lisa promised with mental reservations. Right now, isolation was just what she needed.

'If you're tired, don't wait for the rest of us,' Kyle suggested as if he had sensed her mood. 'No one's going to mind if you have an early night. We've another half-day's travel ahead of us tomorrow.'

'Yes, do,' urged Imogen, a shade too eagerly. 'Can you find your room, or shall I take you?'

'I can find it, thanks.' Lisa kept her tone free of sarcasm. 'I seem to have a good sense of direction.' She came to her feet, smiling at her hostess. 'That was a beautiful meal, Mrs Barrymore. Sorry I couldn't do justice to it.' She avoided Kyle's eyes, too uncertain of her control to risk confrontation. 'Goodnight, everyone.'

The room she had been allocated was at the back of the house overlooking the oval swimming pool and wide, floodlit terrace. There was a small balcony outside her window. She opened the double french doors to let in the soft night air, leaning against the jamb for a moment or two while her head slowly cleared. This house stifled her; the people in it stifled her. Was it going to be any better where she was going tomorrow? She felt so utterly alone, devoid even of the comfort Kyle's presence might have offered her. He had been drawn to her in the beginning: he had said himself how he wanted to make love to her. Only that had been before he knew who she was. She had to stop thinking of him in any emotional sense. Imogen or no Imogen, there was no future in it.

She was in bed and trying to compose herself for sleep when she heard the voices. They were coming from the terrace below, carrying clearly through the open window even though the words themselves were not loudly spoken.

'Kyle, you know how I feel about you. I was under the impression you felt the same.'

'So what makes you doubt it?' The question held a faint impatience. 'I have to get Lisa home.'

'It isn't her home, though, is it? Not really. She's a Hamilton only by marriage.'

'But still half-owner of the estate.'

'She might have some legal claim, but I'm sure it could be taken care of.'

'Buy her off, you mean?'

'Something like that.'

'Except that she still has to recover her memory.'

'She might not do that anyway.'

'She has to.' His tone had harshened. 'I want to know what happened between her and Paul that day. She's the only one who can tell me.'

'And if she doesn't?'

'I'll think about that if and when. In the meantime, I stay put.' A pause, and another change of tone. 'You could always come on over yourself.'

'Seems I'll have to,' with a sigh, 'you're a hard man, Kyle!'

'One track, I'll grant you.' He was smiling now; Lisa could hear it in his voice. 'Let me get this sorted out, then I'll be able to put it behind me.'

Silence fell. Lying there motionless, scarcely breathing, Lisa could imagine the two of them locked in each other's arms—could remember the feel of Kyle's lips and hands. Imogen would know, of course, which was her window. Had she stopped under it deliberately in the hope that their voices would carry on the night air? Yet why should she bother? Kyle was hers; he had made that clear. All he was asking was that she should wait a while.

Unconsciously, her hand had moved to press against the ache under her heart as if in comfort, the back of her thumb brushing the slightly raised shape of the tiny birthmark below the curve of her breast. For the first time, it occurred to her to wonder how Kyle had known about it. Had Paul told him, or had he perhaps caught a glimpse of it some time when she had been wearing a bikini? She had worn brief bikinis: the shape had been etched on her body two years ago. Briefer, certainly, than she would care to wear now. But then she was older now, perhaps a little more circumspect than she would have been at twenty. One thing she couldn't believe herself capable of at any time was the kind of calculation Kyle had suggested. To marry Paul at all she must have loved him—or at the very least imagined herself in love.

There was sound again from below, a soft laugh, a muttered exclamation. Then they were moving away, their footsteps fading until there was nothing left but the gentle whisper of the breeze through the treetops.

Morning brought warm bright sunlight and a sparklingly clear view of the town and harbour. Two cruise ships were already docked, lined up neatly against the wharf. The town itself would be full of tourists, the nearer beaches thronged. Lisa was glad they were leaving, even though her heart quailed at the thought of meeting the rest of the family. So far nothing looked familiar, and there was no guarantee that St Amelia would conjure any memories, but it had to be gone through.

She found Kyle already at breakfast on the terrace, along with herself, the only early riser.

'Boyd is semi-retired,' he said in answer to her light comment. 'That means he can please himself.'

While Imogen was merely tired, perhaps, after a wakeful night, came the ironic thought. There was little doubt that she and Kyle were lovers: the intimacy had been there between them last night. She couldn't afford to let herself care any more. There were more important things to concern her.

'What time do we get to Tortola?' she asked, after ordering cereals and fruit from the white-jacketed man servant.

'Around lunchtime.' Grey eyes studied her as she poured coffee from the fresh pot. 'I gather you slept well? You look less fraught than you did.'

'Perhaps the climate has a soothing effect on the nerves,' Lisa responded blandly. 'Is it like this all year round?'

'Averages around seventy-eight degrees, but the humidity is low due to the trade winds, so it never feels too stinking hot even in the nineties.' His tone was dry. 'There endeth the first lesson. I thought you'd borrowed a Fodor's guide on the area from the library? That would have given all the relative information.'

Lisa shrugged, refusing to be put down. 'It's called making conversation. You've scarcely told me anything about the islands yourself.'

'I didn't want to instil any preconceived ideas. You spent close to three months on St Amelia. With luck, there'll be some recognition when you see it again. Madalyn may decide to come across with the launch, just to give you extra support.'

'She sounds . . . thoughtful.'

'Itching to get in on the act might be nearer the mark.'

The chestnut head lifted sharply. 'You can't possibly believe I might still be pretending!'

'I don't. It was just a figure of speech.' He sounded unapologetic. 'We don't always see eye to eye, that's all.'

'How old is she?' Lisa asked.

'Twenty-five. Same age Paul was when he died.'

A small pulse throbbed at her temple. 'Not planning on getting married herself?'

'Thinking about it.'

'So what's the problem?'

It was Kyle's turn to shrug. 'Lack of enough conviction, I should imagine.'

'Whereas you make up your mind about people and things quickly.'

The irony failed to stir him. 'I consider myself a fair judge of character, yes.'

'And you've never been proved wrong?'

'Let's just say not often.'

'It must make life very easy for you, being that sure.' Her

tone held a bitter note. 'Maybe I needn't look any further than you for the reason my marriage went wrong!'

His eyes narrowed, expression suddenly dangerous. 'What's that supposed to mean, exactly?'

The throbbing had increased, setting her heart hammering in empathy. She seemed to be looking at him from the end of a long, dark tunnel. She took a grip on herself, feeling the world tilt back again on its axis, the sun regain its warmth. 'I'm not sure what it's supposed to mean,' she got out. 'I only know you're against me now. Why did you persuade me to come, Kyle? If you hadn't told me I stood to inherit from Paul I'd never have known about it.'

'You could also say that if I hadn't happened to be driving along Oxford Street at the very moment you chose to throw yourself under my wheels *I'd* never have known about it, but it doesn't alter the facts. You exist, that's what counts.'

She said with bitterness, 'It would have been easier all round if I really had died in that car crash, wouldn't it?'

'Neater,' he agreed on an ironic note. 'Only you didn't and you're here, and no matter what it takes we're going to find out what happened two years ago. Personal feelings don't enter into it.'

Lisa wished she could say the same. Taking a steadying breath, she attempted to match his unemotionalism. 'What will you do with the body in the crypt?'

'Have it moved to another plot, what else? Whoever she is, she's no Hamilton.'

'Someone must have known her.'

'A point that had already occurred to me. She was wearing a wedding ring. As it obviously wasn't one Paul had put there, there should be a husband missing a wife.'

'But not necessarily here on St Thomas.'

'No, but it's a place to start. The missing persons file for that period might throw some light on the matter. We'll call in at the bureau on the way downtown and take a quick look. If she's the reason you left Paul, you might even recognise a name.'

'I might.' Lisa was developing a real headache, spreading across behind her eyes. 'Won't that make us late meeting up with the launch?'

'She'll wait.' He glanced at his watch. 'All the same, as soon as you've eaten we'll get moving.'

'Imogen might not have surfaced by then,' Lisa remarked, and saw a flicker of expression in the eyes looking back at her.

'We already said goodbye. Anyway, she's planning on coming out for a spell.'

'Bringing bell, book and candle?' She regretted the crack the moment it was out, but it was too late to retract. Kyle's lips had curled a fraction.

'She feels nothing but sympathy for you.'

'I don't need sympathy!' This time she let the tartness come through. 'Not from anybody! I've coped with this thing for two years.'

'With Larry's help,' Kyle pointed out. He paused a moment before adding levelly, 'Could you have done it without him?'

The pang that went through her was for all she had left behind. 'If I'd had to, yes.'

'I'll take your word for it.'

The arrival of her cereals and fruit curtailed any further comment for the moment. Lisa ate in silence, aware of his gaze on her. When he did speak again it was on a different note.

'If there's anything you need you'd better get it while we're in Charlotte Amalie. Tortola isn't exactly the shopping mecca of the world.'

'How do you manage on St Amelia?' she asked.

'What we can't grow ourselves we have shipped.'

'Don't you find that rather ... restrictive?'

His smile was dry. 'If you're asking me don't I find the island itself restrictive, the answer is no. I was born there, I aim to die there. Between times, I have a manager capable of running things smoothly whenever I'm away.'

Lisa tried to imagine someone like Imogen settling for that kind of lifestyle. On the face of it, it seemed unlikely. Which meant that one of them was going to have to alter their ideas before anything permanent could come of their relationship. After what he had just said, she couldn't see Kyle being the one—yet who could tell to what lengths a man in love might be prepared to go?

The Barrymores still hadn't put in an appearance when they left the house at nine. Kyle had ordered a taxi to collect them. He had the driver wait while they visited the police station.

His request to see the missing persons files for two years previously met with no opposition. They were even provided with a private cubicle where they could peruse the list. Lisa was both astonished and quite distressed to see the number of names and descriptions, although only three were possibles, taking age, sex and marital status into account. None of them meant anything to her.

Seeing Kyle making a note of addresses, she wondered what his intention might be. He could hardly contemplate a personal approach to each claimant to ask if his wife had been seeing another man before her disappearance. Or could he? For all she knew, he was capable of anything.

Whatever his intention, it apparently wasn't going to be furthered today, because their next stop was down at the harbour where they transferred to the seaplane for their flight to Tortola. The latter took a bare fifteen minutes, putting down in Road Bay on the island's south coast. Whereas from the air St Thomas was shaped like an hourglass with a central spine of mountains, Tortola was irregular and rugged, with little sign, so far as Lisa could see, of commercialised planning. Kyle had informed her that the total population of the British Virgin Islands was only a little over ten thousand, and she could well believe it. Roadtown itself could be navigated in a few minutes.

She was, however, impressed by the launch waiting for them when they reached the wharf. Long and sleek and gleaming white, it would, she thought, have impressed anyone. She nerved herself for her first encounter with the young woman who came out of the cabin to greet them, searching her features for some point of familiarity. Madalyn was a softer counterpart of her brother in looks: the same thick dark hair and grey eyes, the same regular features. Unlike him, however, she was little more than Lisa's own five and a half feet in height, her figure lithe and shapely in the white shorts and T-shirt. The smile on her lips warmed Lisa's heart even if it did nothing to stir her memory.

'I like your hair that style,' the other commented without preamble. 'It used to be half-way down your back.'

'I only had it cut earlier this year,' Lisa acknowledged, wishing she could satisfy the question in her sister-in-law's eyes. It wasn't going to work. Not the way she had hoped. Perhaps nothing ever would.

Madalyn had brought the launch across on her own. She left it to Kyle to take them back, coming to sit with Lisa in the aft well as soon as they cast off.

'I can still hardly believe it,' she confessed. 'When Kyle rang through with the news it was like being hit by a truck!'

'How did your mother take it?' asked Lisa quietly.

The smile took on a wry slant. 'Not well. You survived,

Paul didn't. To her way of thinking, that puts you in the wrong. She'll come round, given time.'

'The way she did before?' She caught the swift change of expression and shook her head. 'Kyle filled me in on a few details. He believes I married Paul for financial reasons. Do you?'

'No.' Madalyn's gaze didn't flicker. 'When you first arrived here you were as starry-eyed as any bride.'

'But only at first.'

'You and Paul scarcely knew each other—and you were neither of you very mature. Perhaps on your own you might have stood a better chance of finding your feet as a couple. Families can be the very devil at times.'

Some members of them, at any rate, Lisa reflected, turning her head to look at Kyle standing at the wheel. He was wearing tailored slacks and matching shirt, emphasising the tapering breadth of shoulder down to narrow waist and hip. His sleeves were rolled to reveal bronzed forearms. A man of integrity, no doubt, only that didn't mean he was incapable of putting a foot wrong. If a wedge had been driven between her and Paul, then Kyle had probably been the one wielding the heaviest mallet. It would explain his reaction this morning when she had suggested much the same thing.

St Amelia came into view as a vague hump on the horizon, gradually extending to a long, low island edged with white beaches and coconut palm and rising to a single range of hills at its eastern end.

'The distillery and dock are down the other end,' Madalyn advised as they headed inshore to a bleached wooden jetty already housing a two-masted yacht. 'The town is a couple of miles or so away over there,' with a sweep of her hand towards the hills, 'we're roughly the same overall size as St John—but I suppose Kyle already told you all this?'

'Some of it,' Lisa acknowledged. 'Only don't let that stop you. I'll need to get orientated.'

'Tomorrow one of us will drive you round. It doesn't take all that long.'

She got to her feet, running nimbly along the outer rim of the cabin superstructure to seize the mooring rope and hop lightly ashore as Kyle brought them alongside the jetty. The latter turned as Lisa came upright.

'Want any help?'

Pride bade her deny it, common sense pointed out the folly of trying to scramble ashore in sandals already insecure on her feet. She should have had more sense than to wear wedged mules, she reflected wryly. Now was no time to rick an ankle. Kyle had taken her agreement for granted, crossing the narrow gap to hold out a hand. Without stopping to think about it, she slipped off the mules and picked them up, stepping on to the seat and then, with his aid, on to the jetty. His skin was warm and dry, his grasp firm. For a brief moment she was close to him—close enough to sense the latent power in the well-muscled frame. Then he had released her and was jumping back into the launch, hoisting the three suitcases.

'Let's go on up to the house,' said Madalyn. 'Kyle will bring the bags.'

'No servants?' asked Lisa on a flippant note as they fell into step.

'We have help around the house, yes.' The other's tone held a faint irony. 'It doesn't mean we can't help ourselves.'

Lisa coloured. 'Sorry. I didn't mean to sound so snide. It's just that it feels so strange knowing I've been here before, yet not recognising a single thing.'

'Yes, it must.' There was sympathy now in Madalyn's

voice. 'Don't try to force it. If it's going to come to you at all it will probably be when you're least expecting it. Some little thing, perhaps.'

'Like another knock on the head, for instance?'

'I wouldn't recommend it.' Kyle had caught them up, the smaller suitcase tucked under an arm, the others swinging from each hand. 'You know, being female doesn't exclude the two of you from carrying anything.'

'It does when there's some big strong male around to do it for us,' retorted his sister, unmoved by the comment.

'Shall I take one from you?' asked Lisa, pausing to look back at him and almost tripping him up in the process.

'I think,' he said drily, 'we'd be as well just carrying on the way we are. I managed this far, I can take it the rest.'

There was a jeep parked on the dirt road just beyond the belt of palm trees. Kyle slung the cases in the back and got behind the wheel, leaving the two girls to share what room was left. Lisa sat beside him only because Madalyn gave her no choice. She would have preferred the rear seat. The cane grew right up to the road edge, tall and lush and stretching as far as eye could see to either hand. So far there was no sense of *déjà vu*—not even a flicker of the curtain. She might well have been setting foot on this island for the very first time for all it meant to her.

After a few hundred yards the road divided, one arm swinging right to cut through the cane, the other continuing on around the perimeter. They took the right-hand fork, running between parallel thickets of yellow-green stalks. Down here the heat was tangible, sticky, the air currents created by their passage no substitute for cooling trade winds. Lisa ran her fingers round the back of her neck to lift the hair away from her nape for a moment or two, but it brought little relief. She could taste the heavy sweetness on her lips.

The cutters were at work farther on. Kyle stopped to have a few words with the towering West Indian who appeared to be in charge. Some of the men paused in their work to stare at the car—or more precisely, at her, she thought. It was obvious they recognised her.

'I had the word passed around,' said Madalyn from the back when they were on their way again. 'Otherwise you might have been taken for a ghost. It'll be a talking point for a few days until the novelty wears off, that's all. Here's Scott,' she added a moment later as another jeep hove into view up ahead. 'He's been working himself to a frazzle while you've been away, Kyle.'

'That's what I pay him for,' returned her brother briefly, slowing to a halt again as they came level with the other vehicle.

Scott, Lisa found, was a man in his early thirties whose light brown hair and pleasant features made little immediate impact. 'Everything under control,' he reported. 'Good to have you back, Kyle.' His gaze shifted to Lisa, taking on a certain restraint in the process. 'You too, Mrs Hamilton.'

'Lisa,' she heard herself saying. 'Call me Lisa.'

There was silence in the car for a moment or two after they drove on. Madalyn was the first to break it. 'Not far now.'

'It's a long way from the beach.' Lisa could think of no other comment.

'Tamarind is built on solid rock,' said Kyle. 'The reason it's still standing. There's a pool for swimming, but no shortage of transport if you prefer the beach.'

'I don't drive,' she said. 'At least . . .'

'You did here.' The statement was flat. 'You don't need any licence.'

'We use horseback a lot too,' put in Madalyn. 'Have you

done any riding this past couple of years?'

'None.' Lisa forced a laugh. 'So many accomplishments I didn't even realise!'

'You hadn't got much past the novice stage, so don't get carried away.' Kyle slowed the vehicle as they came out from the cane belt, pointing across the open tract of land to their right. 'There it is.'

The house lay some half-mile or so distant, semi-concealed by the tall green trees that formed an enclave about it. It was long and two-storeyed, with wide verandas at ground level, that was about all she could tell from where they were now. Kyle drove parallel with it for a few hundred yards before turning on to an unpaved driveway lined with frangipani trees in bloom. This widened on reaching the house to form a complete turning circle before branching off again towards the range of outbuildings to the rear. Stone walls painted a pale shade of pink offset gleaming white woodwork. The veranda looked cool and shady, sheltering the rooms beyond from the full, baking heat of the sun.

'Welcome home again,' Madalyn said softly, watching Lisa's face as she studied the building. 'Not what you expected?'

Lisa shook her head. 'I suppose I'd imagined something pillared and porticoed—as in *Gone With The Wind*.' The last with a faint smile. 'It's the word "plantation" that does it.'

'There was a mansion here before this place was built,' advised Kyle, swinging suitcases from the back of the jeep. 'It was burned down by rioting slaves.'

Lisa glanced at him. 'What happened to the people in it?'

'They were killed. Luckily the son of the house happened to be away at the time, or we wouldn't be here at all.' He was moving towards the veranda steps as he spoke. 'We'll complete the history lesson another time, shall we?'

Catching Madalyn's eye, Lisa warmed to the empathy she saw there. Hamilton or not, this girl was on her side. It helped to know that.

First impressions on stepping through the opened double doors were of spaciousness allied to cool comfort. The hallway was wide and high, tiled underfoot in dark green and white twelve-inch squares and complemented by the green, lemon and white of the ruched window blinds. From the centre rose a fine staircase that branched off right and left to reach galleried landings.

A door to the rear opened to emit a young West Indian dressed casually and comfortably in white cotton slacks and shirt.

'Missis down at the garden house,' he announced. 'Said to bring lunch soon as you got here.' Brown eyes flickered in Lisa's direction, expression curious. 'Want I should take cases up first, Mister Kyle?'

'Yes. And hold the food back for ten minutes while we get cleaned up,' returned the master of the house. To Lisa he added, 'There's a powder-room back there if you want to wash your hands. Save trekking upstairs.'

Lisa felt more in need of a shower and a change from the crumpled linen suit in which she had travelled, but she refrained from saying so. There would be time enough later for relaxing, after she had crossed this next hurdle in the shape of her mother-in-law. Her welcome was going to be far from ecstatic, that much she did know. The question was how to handle the situation.

Madalyn accompanied her to the powder-room, which was decked out more like a lady's boudoir with its chaise-longue and dressing-table.

'We eat most meals down at the garden house when it's just the family,' she volunteered, tidying her hair at the mirror. 'I have to keep reminding myself that it's all new to you.' There was a pause, a slight change of tone. 'Isn't there *any*thing even remotely familiar?'

Lisa shook her head, expression wry. 'I'm beginning to wonder if I really am the person you think I am,' she confessed, then sighed. 'Except that the likelihood of my being someone else is even more remote!'

'It's early days yet,' said Madalyn swiftly. 'And I'm not helping by pushing you, either.' Her grin was appealing. 'Let's both forget it, shall we?'

Lisa smiled back. 'At least that's one way I've got a head start!'

Kyle was waiting for them when they returned to the hall. He had changed his shirt for a short-sleeved cotton one, Lisa noted, feeling her muscles tense anew at the sight of those bare, bronzed arms. They went out via the rear of the house, passing the kitchen premises on the way. Two staff, at least, thought Lisa, hearing voices. She wondered if they were talking about her homecoming.

While the front of the house had been laid out mostly to grass, landscaping at the back was a tropical paradise of lush greens shot through with the exotic colours of flamboyant and hibiscus. Bougainvillaea spilled over old stone walls and arches. Through one of the latter they came upon the pool, set clear of overhanging trees within an oval of sun-bleached paving. Now covered in creeper, the remains of the old mill had a semi-circular pergola built out from its base almost to the pool edge. Under it was set table and chairs, the former ready-laid for a meal. The woman sitting there turned her head as the three of them approached, but made no attempt to rise. With her faded fair hair and delicate features, she bore little immediate resemblance to either of her two offspring.

'Did you see Samuel?' she demanded. 'I told him to serve lunch as soon as you got here.'

'It's coming,' soothed her daughter. 'Say hello to Lisa, Mother.'

Lisa summoned a smile as the glance shifted her way, feeling it fade again before the unconcealed animosity. 'I'm not going to pretend I'm glad to see you again,' said the older woman. 'If it wasn't for you I might still have my son!'

'That's hardly fair,' interjected Madalyn before Lisa could recover her balance. 'She wasn't even there when it happened.'

'Perhaps because she knew it was going to happen.'

Kyle moved abruptly. 'I think that's far enough.'

'No.' Lisa was pale but resolute. 'It's best to get it all out in the open. You think I might have somehow caused the car to crash, Mrs Hamilton, is that what you're saying?'

Pale blue eyes flickered at the directness of the counter-attack. 'Paul was a good driver,' she rallied. 'He . . .'

'Paul was a fast driver,' cut in her elder son levelly. 'The skid marks proved that he had to have been doing around seventy when he hit that bend.'

'Due to possible brake failure, they said at the inquest.'

'Possible, not probable. They were giving him the benefit of the doubt. And let's leave it there, shall we?' He drew out a chair, the eyes meeting Lisa's devoid of expression. 'Have a seat.'

Short of walking away, there was little else she could do but obey the injunction. She felt too tense to eat, her mouth dry as a bone. The accusation was ridiculous, of course. Kyle had said she had driven around the island when she was here before, but that didn't make her a mechanic capable of sabotaging a braking system.

Samuel arrived bearing lunch on a covered trolley, leaving them to help themselves from an array of cold cuts and salads and tempting savouries. From a concealed refrigerator behind the built-in bar at the rear of the pergola, Kyle took a bottle of chilled white wine and filled all four glasses before taking a seat between Lisa and his mother.

'I'll be spending the afternoon across at the plant,' he announced. 'One or two things I want to sort out.'

An excuse to stay out of the way, Lisa reckoned, concentrating on her plate. She couldn't really blame him all that much. The atmosphere alone made her want to cut and run. Trying to reason with Mrs Hamilton was an obvious waste of time and effort. She would just have to let her come round in her own good time—if she ever did.

It was Madalyn who got them through the meal by finding uncontroversial subjects to talk about. Elaine Hamilton was the only one who remained silent throughout, expression brooding. She would stay where she was, she said when Kyle had left and Madalyn suggested a return to the house. Lisa she simply ignored.

'I had no idea she was going to go that far,' Madalyn apologised wryly as soon as they were alone. 'It must have been building up since Kyle phoned through with the news. When Paul died she seemed to lose interest in everything. For the past two years she's spent most of her time down there in the garden house. It was one of his favourite places too—when he was here.'

Lisa glanced her way. 'You're saying he didn't spend too much time on the island?'

'No more than he absolutely had to.' Slim shoulders lifted. 'Paul was all for living life to the full. St Amelia hardly provided enough diversion. Kyle handed over half the estate in the hope of giving him some sense of responsibility, but all it did do was increase his spending power. He'd been doing Europe for three months when he met you. He didn't even bother to tell us he was coming home, much less that he was bringing a wife.'

Lisa said softly, 'Shock number one for your mother.'

'For all of us. Paul wasn't cut out for marriage. Not as he was then, anyway. I think he did it just to show Kyle.' She caught herself up, added swiftly, 'Well, perhaps not only for that reason.'

'It's all right.' Lisa kept her tone level. 'I'd already reached the conclusion that he didn't do it for love. Kyle believes he married me because I wouldn't let him have me any other way.'

'It's possible that came into it,' Madalyn acknowledged after a moment, 'but I doubt if you used sex as leverage.'

'How can you be sure? How can I be sure, if it comes to that?'

'Because it's only your memory you've lost, not your basic character. If you couldn't do a thing now, you couldn't have done it then.'

'That's what I keep trying to tell myself.' Lisa felt only slightly comforted. 'On the face of it, I might never know.'

'You've scarcely given it a chance yet.'

'But the possibility has to be considered.' She hesitated before voicing the next question. 'Kyle says he took me sailing with him a couple of times. Did Paul go too?'

'Unlikely. He had no interest in boats.' The smooth brow had puckered a little. 'I don't recall any private sailing expeditions. Must have been when I was away myself.'

'Seeing your fiancé?'

'Tod isn't my fiancé. And I didn't even know him then.' Her tone lightened. 'You'll be able to meet him next week. He's coming to stay for a few days.'

Lisa tried to match the change of mood. 'It's going to be quite a house party if Imogen arrives too.'

'Imogen, coming here?' The other sounded surprised. 'She was bored to tears the last time.'

A small price to pay when it was Kyle himself who

wanted her there, reflected Lisa achingly. She herself
would be the odd man out.

They went straight upstairs on reaching the house. The
room Lisa was to occupy was at the rear, overlooking the
gardens, shaded by a tamarind tree whose branch tips
brushed the window panes. A hand-crocheted spread lay
across the double bed, the blue of the underlay picked up in
carpet and curtains. Built-in wardrobes lined the whole of
one wall.

'Not the room you shared with Paul,' said Madalyn,
guessing her thoughts as she hesitated in the doorway.
'That's across on the other landing. You don't have to go in
there at all, unless you feel you want to.'

'Not just now,' Lisa acknowledged gratefully. 'What I'd
really like is to have a shower and lie down for an hour. I
was up early this morning, and I still feel jet-lagged.'

'Good idea.' Madalyn walked over and opened the end
door in the wall of supposed wardrobes. 'Here's your
bathroom. Only small, but it's functional. En suite wasn't
thought of when this place was built, so we sacrificed a
portion of each bedroom where possible. Let no man say we
lack the refinements on St Amelia!'

'Are you happy here?' asked Lisa impulsively, sensing
cynicism behind the light remark. 'Don't you find it a bit
confining?'

The dark head moved from side to side. 'It's easy enough
to get away when I feel like a change. Of course, there may
come a time when I'll have to leave, unless I want to finish
up an old maid.' She was smiling as she said it, but the smile
didn't reach her eyes. 'I'll leave you to it, then. If you want
anything there's a bell-push by the bed.' At the room door
she paused again to add, 'By the way, my mother always
takes a siesta between two-thirty and six, so you can use the

pool then, if you feel like it, without having to face the inquisition.'

That was worth knowing, Lisa conceded as the door closed. The last thing she wanted was to find herself alone with her mother-in-law. Her suitcases were standing by the bed. Reluctantly, she hoisted one of them up to begin unpacking. There was no feeling of permanency about this homecoming—no feeling of any kind. The only home she knew was back in London. Right now she would have given just about anything to be back there.

CHAPTER FOUR

IT was almost five when she awoke from a fitful, restless sleep that left her unrefreshed either in body or mind. The sunlight filtering into the room was full and golden. Voices sounded from outside in the garden, fading away as if the owners had moved on round the side of the house. Apart from the rustling of the breeze through the tree branches and distant bird calls, all was quiet again.

Sitting up, Lisa pushed a heavy hand through lank hair, grimacing at the sticky feel. She had meant to shower before taking a nap, but lethargy had overruled her. The swim Madalyn had mentioned was a temptation. It was doubtful if they would eat dinner before seven-thirty, so there would be time to wash her hair and dry it first.

Pulling on a white suit and plain towelling robe, she made her way downstairs. One of the arched doors stood open, revealing part of a large and lovely living-room in which the same colours of green and white and pale coral had been used to good effect. A room to relax in, thought Lisa, viewing it at closer quarters from the doorway. Some of the furnishings looked old enough to have been here since the house was built, though scarcely lacking in comfort because of it.

On impulse, she moved further into the room, running a hand over fine, polished wood, fingering fabrics, trying through her sense of touch to conjure up some picture in her mind. Only there was nothing: she hadn't really expected there would be. This room, this house, they were part of a past to which she had never belonged. Where was the incentive to remember?

She reached the baby grand piano, looking out through the window as she idly fingered the keys. The embrasures showed the thickness of the walls. With such insulation there would never be any need for air-conditioning even on the hottest days. Already the sun was low in the sky. If she didn't go for that swim soon it would be too late. Pleasant swimming in the dark though, with only the cicadas and fireflies for company—the water silky on the skin, silvered by moonlight, the tinkle of music in her ears ... Heart jerking, she looked down at the finger still pressing a key. She had been picking out a tune just then: it still ran through her mind. Nothing she knew, she was certain: she hadn't even been aware of what she was doing.

I can play, she thought suddenly staring at the keyboard. I know where and what each note is! She sat down tentatively on the stool, flexing her fingers before placing them in position, beginning to play, haltingly at first, then with slowly increasing confidence as instinct took over. No concert pianist, for sure, a part of her mind assessed, but competent enough. She kept the soft pedal down so that the sound wouldn't carry too far, almost unable to believe that she was doing what she was doing. At no time during the past two years had she been aware of any musical talent, but then this was the first time she had touched a piano. What other skills might she possess could she only remember!

She was trembling too much to finish the piece. Sitting there with her hands resting on the keys, she closed her eyes and allowed her body to sag. It was no use: nothing else was coming through. So she could play the piano. What difference did it make?

'You used to amuse yourself in here quite a lot,' said Kyle from the doorway, jerking her out of her thoughts again.

'And annoy everyone else?' she managed.

'I didn't say that.' His brows lifted as she stood up and

moved abruptly away from the instrument. 'Change of plan?'

'I was on my way to the pool,' she said on a faintly defensive note. 'The door was open, so I came in to have a look, that's all.'

'You don't need to excuse yourself,' he responded with a tilt of his lip. 'The house is half yours too.' There was a brief pause before he added softly, 'That tune you were playing . . .'

Her heart began a sudden irregular tattoo. 'You recognised it?'

'I've heard it before, yes.'

'Where?'

Grey eyes considered her, expression indeterminate. 'I thought you might tell me.'

'If I could I'd hardly be asking,' she pointed out. 'I don't know what it's called, I don't know where it came from. I only know it keeps running through my head.'

'It's like that sometimes.' His tone was evasive. 'If you're still planning on going down to the pool I'll join you. Just give me five minutes.'

Lisa stayed where she was, looking after him as he crossed the hall to the stairs. Only when he was out of sight did she stir herself into movement. Kyle knew where the pool was. He didn't need taking by the hand. She didn't really want his company, but she could hardly have said so. The alternative was simply not to be there.

Except that it didn't work out that way, because she found herself heading for the back door regardless. If she was going to occupy the same house she had to make some effort towards achieving a better relationship, she reasoned. That wasn't going to happen if she spent all her time avoiding being alone with him. The effect he had on her was something she was going to have to learn to live with— if she stayed.

She was in the water when he arrived. Stripping off his short robe, he dived in cleanly, surfacing at her side as she stretched out to float for a while. His body was everything she had imagined it to be: she could still see him poised there for that brief instant, outlined against the deepening blue of the sky. A man for all seasons: where had that line come from? Whatever, it fitted him.

'Why didn't you wait?' he asked, smoothing excess moisture from his hair with one hand as he trod water.

'I didn't realise you wanted me to wait.' She had her eyes closed. 'Was everything all right at the plant?'

'Running smoothly. In Scott's hands I wouldn't expect anything else.'

Then why the hurry to check up on him? Lisa wondered. Aloud she said, 'He's obviously been with you for some time.'

'Almost three years. He joined us not long before you did.'

'Because you couldn't rely on Paul to honour his commitment?'

'That came into it.' There was a pause, a change of tone. 'Try not to let my mother's attitude cut too deeply. She hasn't been herself since Paul died.'

'She obviously thought the world of him.' Lisa had come upright, keeping herself afloat with small movements of her arms and legs. The sun was behind Kyle's head, sparkling the droplets of water still clinging to the thickness of his hair. 'More than she did of you and Madalyn?' she added softly.

His smile was dry. 'Paul was the only one of us to take after her side of the family—where colouring was concerned, at least.'

'That surely shouldn't make so much difference.'

'In most circumstances, perhaps not.' He studied her a moment, then seemed to come to some decision. 'He wasn't a Hamilton by birth.'

Lisa's brow furrowed. 'I'm not sure I understand.'

'It's simple enough. She had an affair with another man. Paul was the result.'

Shock clouded her mind for a moment or two. 'Your father knew?' she got out at length.

'From the first.' The strong mouth had a twist. 'He loved her enough to forgive her, and accept the baby as his own.'

Her back had come up against the side rail. She reached out both arms and grasped it, needing the support. 'Did I know all this before?'

'It's doubtful.' He moved in after her, drawing himself up out of the water to sit on the poolside. 'Paul never knew himself.'

'Then why tell me now?' she demanded.

'Because I want you to make allowances for her. When Paul brought you back with him she felt you'd robbed her of the only thing she could really call her own. Madalyn and I are Hamiltons through and through. We were independent from a very early age. Paul was different. He relied on her. It was hard enough for her to take when he went off to school, even more so when he got the travel bug. She lived for him coming home.'

Lisa said softly, 'So that's why you made him a partner.'

'Don't give me too much credit. I needed help with the plantation. Maybe I hoped to kill two birds with one stone.' The touch on her shoulder, light though it was, made her flinch. 'You're shivering. Better come on out and get something on.' He was getting to his feet as he spoke. 'Give me your hand.'

'I can manage, thanks.' Not for anything was she going to risk close contact again. 'I'll use the ladder.'

Kyle walked over and secured her robe from the lounger where she had left it, holding it ready for her to slip in her arms when she reached the side, his grey eyes enigmatic.

Lisa turned her back, feeling his hands through the material as they rested for a brief moment before releasing the garment. Once, not so very long ago, she had allowed those same hands free range of her body; the muscles of her inner thighs trembled at the thought. She could smell the sea again in her nostrils, hear the sound of breaking surf, see in her mind's eye the wide sweep of his shoulders blocking out the sunlight . . .

The vision faded almost before it had formed, sinking back into the depths of her mind. She groped blindly for a seat on the lounger.

'Are you all right?' Kyle's voice seemed to becoming from a long distance away. 'Lisa . . .'

'It's nothing. Just a touch of the sun, perhaps.' The strength was slowly coming back into her limbs. 'I should have worn a hat this morning.' She lifted her head, taking in the muscular length of his legs, the leanness of hip in the tautly stretched black trunks, dragging her eyes upward to reach his face with a sense of desperation. 'I'll be fine in a minute. Just let me sit here.'

'I'm not asking you to move.' He sat down himself on the neighbouring lounger, eyes narrowed as he watched her. 'Want to talk about it?'

'There's nothing much to tell.' She had control of herself again now. 'For a second or two I was on the verge of remembering something, that's all. It's happened before— like wakening out of a dream you can't keep a hold on.'

'It can't have been a pleasant dream to make you look the way you did.'

'No.' She wished he would leave it alone. 'You didn't have much of a swim.'

'I can swim any time,' he said. 'Why don't you lie back and relax? It won't be dark for another half-hour or so. I'll stay and keep you company.'

She wanted to tell him to go on ahead without her, but

she doubted if he would let her stay here alone. She needed time to think, to straighten herself out. Her mind was in turmoil.

Hands clasped behind his head, he stretched out on the lounger beside her, apparently content to let silence take over. It was left to her to say slowly, 'Why the change of heart, Kyle? Up to a few hours ago you felt much the same about me as your mother.'

'Not quite. It never occurred to me that you might have been responsible for arranging the accident.' He seemed to be considering his words very carefully. 'It was listening to her that made me realise how unbalanced my own attitude was. Whatever happened between you and Paul, it was over two years ago. Perhaps we should leave it there. Start again from here.'

'What about the woman who was in the car?' Lisa asked after a moment.

'The police can handle it.' The dark head turned in her direction when she failed to make immediate response. 'We have to face the fact that you might never recover your memory. It's been known to happen. Do you think you can live with that possibility?'

'I can try,' she said.

'That's the spirit.' There was just the faintest hint of irony in his voice. 'One thing you were never lacking in. Tomorrow I'll show you your inheritance in full. It's quite extensive. How does it feel to be a woman of property?'

'No different,' she confessed. 'Probably because I can't convince myself I've any claim.'

'I'm no philanthropist, believe me. A fool, sometimes, maybe.'

'Because you told me at all?'

'I was thinking more in terms of past mistakes.'

Lisa said softly, 'I shouldn't have thought you ever made many.'

'Every man's allowed his quota.'

'And woman?'

He turned his head to look at her, an odd expression in his eyes. 'You're starting with a clean slate. Not many of us get that chance.'

'I'll try to keep it that way,' she assured him, and knew it was already too late. Her biggest mistake of all was in coming back here.

Elaine Hamilton took dinner in her room, much to Lisa's relief. Eaten by lamplight, the meal itself was both casual and enjoyable. The plantation manager had joined them, apparently by invitation. He had a bungalow of his own a couple of miles away, Lisa learned, and spent a lot of his spare time collecting and cataloguing the wonderfully hued butterflies with which the island abounded. A quiet man, with an inner togetherness she found particularly enviable.

'He doesn't talk much about his past,' Madalyn said later, when they had left the two men together over a chess board. 'There was a wife once, that much I do know. Whatever she did to him, it seems to have put him off women for life!'

Lisa glanced at her curiously. 'He doesn't strike me as being a woman hater.'

'Oh, not in the everyday sense. Try getting close to him and it's a different story.'

'You mean you have tried?'

Madalyn's shrug made light of the words. 'I never could resist a challenge.'

'Then you met Tod and lost interest?'

'I met Tod, yes.' Abruptly she changed the subject. 'You and Kyle were on better terms tonight.'

'His doing,' Lisa agreed. 'He thinks we should forget about what happened and start over.'

'He does?' She sounded surprised. 'It isn't like Kyle to change tack. When I spoke to him on the phone he was all for turning over every last stone. Anyway, it's a relief. All he needs to do now is persuade mother to see it the same way. At least she's showing some sign of life. She's been like a zombie the last two years.'

If nothing else they could thank her for that, reflected Lisa. All the same, it was going to be difficult getting through to the woman, if it could be managed at all.

They had been strolling in the gardens, coming out now on a circular patio built around another of the tamarind trees from which the house took its name. The incessant strumming of the cicadas had become part of the background by now, scarcely noticed. Lisa sniffed pleasurably at the mingled scents of jasmine and night-blooming cactus.

'It's so peaceful!' she exclaimed.

'Make the most of it,' Madalyn advised. 'We often have visitors turning up.'

'Not everyone finds it so boring, then?'

'Meaning Imogen? If she wants Kyle she'll have to reconcile herself to spending at least some of her time here.' Cynicism tinged her voice. 'Women still make all the sacrifices when it comes to love.'

'You think she is?' Lisa tried to make the question casual. 'In love with him, I mean.'

'As close as someone like her is going to come to it.'

'I thought the two of you were friends,' with a swift sideways glance.

'We don't have a lot in common, although I'm sure she has her good points—being of a genereous nature. Me, that is, not her. She has to have something to attract Kyle. He's not generally drawn to light-weights. Did she say just when she was coming over?'

'Not to the day.'

'Well, I don't suppose it matters. We're not short of room.' Madalyn was making no attempt to continue their stroll. 'I don't know about you, but I've had enough moonlight for one night,' she said now. 'Feel like a drink?'

'I don't mind.' Lisa turned with her to head back in the direction they had come, walking in silence for a few steps before saying tentatively, 'Are there any photographs of Paul still around?'

'I'm not sure,' admitted the other. 'We were never much for family snapshots. Mother may have one tucked away somewhere.'

'I'd hate to ask her.'

'I don't blame you.' Madalyn looked suddenly thoughtful. 'You know, I don't believe your things were ever gone through properly. They'll still be stored in one of the attics.'

'*My* things?' Lisa was startled.

'Well, I didn't do any throwing out, and I'm fairly sure no one else did. There's stuff up there that belonged to my great-grandmother. Now why didn't I think of that before?' She quickened her footsteps. 'You never know what you might find!'

No, Lisa thought with sudden reluctance, you don't. 'Shouldn't we leave it till morning?' she suggested. 'It's getting a bit late to start looking tonight.'

'There's no time like the present.' Madalyn was determined. 'You want to know about yourself, don't you?'

She wasn't even sure of that any more, Lisa acknowledged, then pushed the thought to the back of her mind. 'Yes, of course,' she said. 'I'm coming.'

The attics were reached via a narrow staircase from the upper floor. Madalyn switched on a light in the first one to reveal a veritable treasure house of bric-a-brac and bits of furniture. There were several old trunks. Opening one of them, she drew out a dress made of fine silk taffeta in delicate shades of grey, spreading wide the long full skirts.

'Can you imagine having to wear something like this just to go down to dinner? Or this?' fishing out a flower-strewn bonnet. 'A lady kept her skin white in those days.' She put the things back, looking around with thoughtfully pursed lips. 'Now where would they have put your stuff?'

'We could ask them,' Lisa suggested, assuming she meant the house staff. 'There's always tomorrow.'

Madalyn wasn't listening. Her gaze had come to rest on a wooden packing-case pushed in under the curve of the roof. 'That looks reasonably new. Shall we take a look?'

'I suppose so.' Lisa was constrained, wishing she had never mentioned the subject. She hadn't had time to adjust to being here at all yet, much less to making new discoveries. Whatever was in that case, it belonged to someone else, not to her.

There was no padlock, just an ordinary clasp. Throwing back the lid. Madalyn made a sound of satisfaction. 'This is it! I recognise the brush set. Kyle gave it to you on your twenty-first.'

Drawn despite herself, Lisa moved to view the contents of the box at closer quarters. It was almost full of neatly folded clothing, with a few loose items laid on top of the pile. The brush set Madalyn had spoken of was backed with intricately worked filigree silver, tarnished now from two years of neglect. She reached out a nerveless hand and picked up the mirror, turning it over to see her face reflected, green eyes so dark they looked almost black. April the fourteenth: she would have been on the island more than two months by then.

'Did I have a party?' she asked.

'No. As a matter of fact, I was away at the time. You never told anyone about it, you see. Kyle only found out by accident.' Madalyn was watching her with faint anxiety. 'Are you OK? You've gone pale.'

'Too much build up of expectation, I expect. I think a

part of me anticipated total recall once I saw inside this thing.'

'Then why the reluctance?'

Lisa's smile was wry. 'Because I might not like what I find if I do remember.'

'*When* you remember. You've got to think positively.' Madalyn reached out and took the mirror from her, weighing it in her hand. 'You should have these down to use. They're too good to leave hidden away.'

'I already have a hairbrush.' Lisa glanced down into the box again. 'I had quite a wardrobe, didn't I? Bought here, or did I arrive with as much?'

'The two of us made a couple of shopping expeditions to Charlotte Amalie.'

'Was I spending my own money, or Paul's?'

'I never asked.' Madalyn touched a pale blue silk sleeve. 'I remember that little number. You looked a million dollars in it. Your measurements don't seem to have altered. They should all still fit. It's a pity to let them go to waste.'

If the dress she had been found in was anything to go by, her present wardrobe bore little comparison, Lisa was bound to concede. All the same, she felt no desire to abandon it.

'Later,' she said. 'Right now we're supposed to be looking for a photograph.'

'So we were.' A leather writing-case lay under the silver-backed brush. She picked it up and handed it over. 'Take a peek in there while I delve a bit deeper. Whoever packed this lot didn't do it with any organisation.'

'I don't suppose they thought it necessary,' Lisa responded, clicking open the catch on the leather case. Something small and dark fell out on to the floor. She bent to pick it up, barely glancing at it. 'Just a button. There's nothing in here except paper and envelopes.'

'What you might expect, I suppose.' Madalyn gave a sudden exclamation, emerging triumphant from the depths of the box holding a silver frame in her hand. 'Here we are! Both of you together.'

Lisa had to force herself to take the frame from her sister-in-law. Of the two faces gazing back at her, only one was in any way familiar. She looked so young and happy, she thought achingly. The man with his arm resting lightly across her shoulders was slimly built and possessed of rakish good looks beneath the sweep of blond hair. They were both wearing ski suits and holding upended skis. Behind their heads could be seen the wires and chairs of a lift stretching away up the mountainside.

'I can't imagine I ever went up there,' she commented after a moment, unable to think of anything else to say.

'By all accounts you shouldn't have done.' Madalyn sounded disappointed, as if she had been anticipating some sudden flood of revelation. 'Paul told us you were only a comparative beginner when he first saw you, but daring enough to take him on when he challenged you to tackle one of the longer runs. The fact that you could have killed yourself wouldn't have occurred to him, of course.'

'It obviously didn't occur to me either,' Lisa said, still gazing at the photograph. 'It's more than I'd do these days, I'm sure.'

'Oh, I don't know. Given the same circumstances, and a man you wanted to impress . . .' Madalyn left it there, adding on a more sober note, 'You're probably right, at that. We all get less daring as we get older—or more sensible. Anyway, that proved a dead loss. It doesn't stir a thing, does it?'

Lisa shook her head. 'Sorry.'

'Lord, don't apologise! You didn't choose to get landed with all this. I suppose,' she added on a rueful note, 'we should stop trying so hard—or I should, anyway. Too much pressure might have the opposite effect. Are you going to put that back?'

Lisa hesitated, not really sure what she wanted. 'It's perhaps best not to push it,' she agreed after a moment, 'but it's no use hiding from it either. I'll need to go through everything.'

'Fine. We'll get Samuel and Josh to fetch the box down first thing in the morning. You can have it in your room till you've decided what you want to keep and what you don't.' She closed the lid down, dusting off her hands. 'About time somebody came up here and sorted the whole lot out, before the ceilings cave in with the weight!'

'You'd be getting rid of a lot of history,' Lisa reminded her. 'I'm sure the ceilings can stand it.'

'You're probably right.' The glance was warm. 'I'm glad you're back, Lisa. I missed you.'

They found the two men talking comfortably together over drinks.

'Scott's game,' Kyle acknowledged, getting up to fetch their requirements from the bar.

'Only because your mind wasn't on it,' returned the other man. 'You were definitely thinking about something else tonight.'

Or someone, thought Lisa. Imogen was here in spirit if not in body. She accepted the glass he brought her without looking at him, too afraid of what she might give away if she allowed their eyes to meet.

'So what have you two been doing with yourselves for the last hour or so?' he asked casually, taking his seat again.

It was Madalyn who answered. 'We were up in the attic. Lisa's things are still stored up there.'

'I gather you had no luck.' Scott sounded quietly sympathetic.

Lisa smiled at him. 'Not yet, but I'm filling in some

pieces. Who knows, I might wake up some morning and it will all be there!'

'In the meantime, you're in good hands.'

Kyle stirred restlessly. 'I can smell rain coming. Maybe we should go on up to the house before it gets started.'

The other man shook his head. 'If you're right, and you usually are, I'd as soon get on home before it breaks.' He drained his glass and stood up, lean and fit in the casual shirt and slacks. 'Thanks for the game, Kyle, even if you did give it away.'

'I'll walk with you as far as the car,' Madalyn offered unexpectedly, leaving her own glass untouched. 'I'm not really in the mood for this, anyway.'

Kyle watched the two of them disappear out of sight among the shrubbery, cynicism in the line of his mouth. 'I thought she'd given up in that direction,' he observed, as if speaking his thoughts aloud. He brought his attention back to immediate company as Lisa made a movement. 'You've time to finish your drink.'

She wasn't in the mood for it either, but she subsided again. 'What did you mean just now?' she asked after a moment.

Kyle shrugged. 'She's been trying off and on for three years to get under that shell of his, without much result. The trouble with my sister is she can't reconcile herself to defeat.'

'You think Scott might be the reason she can't make up her mind about Tod?'

'I'd say it was more because she'd have to leave St Amelia if she did marry him.'

'But if she loved him, surely . . .'

His lips twisted again. 'You think love solves everything?'

'No,' she acknowledged, 'but I think it's an essential part of a relationship.'

'So is compatibility. She has a lot more in common with Tod Sherman than she has with Scott.'

'Not enough, apparently, to swing the scales in his favour.' She added lightly, 'He doesn't sound the type to consider that name change if you fail to produce any male offspring, but then neither, I imagine, is Scott, so you'd be stuck either way.'

'Which leaves me with little alternative,' he agreed drily. 'Lucky I'm not in my dotage yet!'

What kind of mother would Imogen make? wondered Lisa with a pang. Would she even have considered that far ahead? It was difficult to imagine that model-girl figure of hers burgeoning with child—harder still to think of its being Kyle's. No, not harder, just more painful. What right did she have to begrudge someone else that experience? Kyle was her brother-in-law. She had to think of him that way and no other.

The gin and lime juice she had asked for was stronger than her usual mix. She coughed now as the spirit caught the back of her throat, groping for a handkerchief. There was a tinkle of something falling as she pulled the latter from her pocket. Kyle bent to retrieve the object, cupping it in his palm to look at it under the lamplight.

'Coming apart?' he asked expressionlessly.

The button she had picked up from the attic floor, Lisa remembered. 'It fell out when we opened the box with my things in,' she said. 'I must have slipped it into my pocket.'

He dropped the disc into her own outstretched palm with a dismissive gesture. 'Hardly a collector's item.'

That assessment Lisa was bound to agree with on closer inspection. Small, and navy blue in colour, the button was of the kind that might grace the sleeve of a blazer or other casual jacket. No doubt she would find the garment to which it belonged if she checked through the contents of the packing-case. No, *when*, she corrected herself, recalling

Madalyn's advice. It was time she stopped shying away from things.

'You said something about showing me the island tomorrow,' she murmured, putting the button back into her pocket. 'Will it take long?'

'You can count on most of the day if we're going to do the thing properly,' he returned. 'We can take a packed lunch.'

Her chin lifted a fraction. 'Complete with champagne?'

'Not unless you especially want some.' He hadn't turned a hair. 'Do you?'

Lisa shook her head, already regretting the tart retort. 'I don't think I'll ever drink the stuff again.'

'Because you hold it responsible for what happened between us?' This time it was he who shook his head, the mockery as much self-directed. 'We never got round to drinking any. I wonder what might have happened if that birthmark hadn't given you away?'

'With luck, I'd have come to my senses before it was too late.' There was a tight constriction in her chest. 'If I'd known who you were, of course . . .'

'You wouldn't have felt the same attraction?'

She gave a sudden little shiver. 'I thought you said the rain was coming.'

'So it is. The temperature always drops a few points ahead of it.' Kyle got to his feet. 'Leave the rest of that. You can always have another up at the house if you want it.'

The first drops came as they reached the shelter of the veranda. Within seconds there was a regular deluge, cascading rivulets from the sloping roof. Madalyn was already curled up in one of the cane chairs, a fresh drink to hand.

'You only just made it,' she observed. 'I'd visions of sending Samuel down with an umbrella.' She added, for Lisa's benefit, 'It won't last long, and it'll be bone dry again by morning. We'll sit inside if you'd rather.'

'I think I'll go on up,' Lisa told her. 'I haven't quite finished unpacking yet.' Her smile emcompassed them both. 'See you in the morning.'

Her room was a haven: the one place where she could be alone with her thoughts. Not that the latter were by any means clear cut. Kyle was the stumbling block; Kyle, who had been attracted to the girl he knew as Adria Morris because she looked like his dead brother's wife, yet had, by his own account, distrusted and despised the younger Lisa. It didn't make any sense.

And what of her own emotions? Was it possible that what she felt for Kyle now was simply an extension of what she had felt then? Yet Paul had been her husband, the man she was supposed to have loved. Unless it was true that she had married him for purely mercenary reasons. How could she be sure of *any*thing?

CHAPTER FIVE

THERE was little change in Elaine Hamilton's attitude over the following few days, although she at least took her place at the meal table again. Ignored for the most part, Lisa tried not to let it upset her too much. Like it or not, eventually the other woman would have to learn to accept the situation. It was only to be hoped that the time would be sooner rather than later, for everyone's sake.

In the meantime there was so much else to occupy her mind. The promised tour of the island proved a fascinating, if unfruitful, experience. Confined to the western corner, the industrial side of the business spread over several acres. Kyle took her through the whole process of rum production, from the pressing out of the cane juice, through fermentation by the addition of yeast enzymes, and subsequent distillation in vast, steam-heated stills to draw off the raw liquor. This was then stored in oak casks and left to mature for a minimum of three years before eventual bottling and despatch. A deep-water harbour provided access for the cargo ships.

At the opposite end of the island, and built around a natural bay, the town itself was larger than anticipated: a collection of red-brick bungalows each contained within its own bright little garden and spread along several unpaved streets. Tropical evergreens provided shade, creating dappled patterns on white walls as the trade winds rustled their branches. There was a church complete with bell tower, a general store, and a meeting hall which was used during the day as a schoolroom for the younger children, the older ones travelling to Tortola for their educational needs.

The people who lived on the island were mostly descendents of the slaves his ancestors had imported, Kyle explained when Lisa expressed her interest in that distant past. The rest of the workforce came over from Tortola on a daily basis. Tamarind was one of the few plantations to survive abolition, chiefly because production had been turned over from raw sugar to rum.

'Do you think your great, great whatever grandfathers were good to their slaves?' she asked him, trying to visualise the day and age.

His smile was dry. 'If they'd all been that good the old house might still have been standing. There are a few relics of the old days left in one of the outhouses. I'll show you them some time, though I warn you, they're not for the squeamish.'

'The son who escaped the riot,' she said, 'how did he carry on afterwards?'

'He brought in government aid to quell the rebels, then set about rebuilding. Whether he treated the people any better for the warning is open to conjecture. In those days the blacks weren't even counted as being human.'

'But there were no more riots?'

'Apparently not. Somewhere along the line there had to be a build-up of loyalty in order for any of them to be willing to stay on and work the plantation after they were made free men.'

'Perhaps some of them had the sense to see they'd be better off here where they knew there was a living to be made rather than taking their chances outside.'

'Probably. The same attitude that keeps families here

today.' They were sitting beside the pool after a late afternoon swim. Madalyn was still in the water. He added casually, 'Did you go through your old things yet?'

Her mood took a dive. 'Yes. Not with any far-reaching conclusions, though. I thought I might find some personal papers—a diary, even—only there was nothing of that nature.'

'You think it likely you might have kept a diary?'

'I'm not sure. Just an idea, that's all.' She had her knees bent up on the poolside, her arms wrapped about them. She said slowly, 'If I took everything like that with me when I went to St Thomas it can only have been because I knew I wasn't coming back.'

The tone was measured. 'I wasn't around when you left.'

'But you knew Paul and I were having problems. You said we were all washed up.'

'So it seemed.' He ground out the end of the cheroot he had been smoking into the ashtray at his side and reached for the robe lying ready over the lounger at his back, getting to his feet to pull it on. 'I'm going on up. I've a couple of calls to make. See you later.'

Lisa watched him stride away, parallel lines creasing her brows. He wasn't telling her everything, that was almost certain, yet what could she do about it? They had been doing so well these last few days. She hesitated to spoil that tenuous relationship by attempting to force any issues—especially when she wasn't even sure what it was she wanted to know.

'He took off a bit sharpish, didn't he?' commented Madalyn, pulling herself on to the tiled edge.

'He said he had some calls to make,' Lisa told her.

'One of them to his lady love, no doubt. Has he said any more about this visit of hers?'

Lisa registered the pang without surprise. 'Not to me.'

'Well, with any luck she'll change her mind. I'm surprised it ever got this far at all.'

'How long has he known her?' Lisa tried to keep the question casual.

'Oh, about six months, I suppose. Not much more.'

'I suppose there have been plenty of other women friends in the past.'

'Not as many as you might think. Well, not recently, anyway. What he really needs is one capable of switching from one lifestyle to another, the way he does himself. St Amelia might be his home, but he likes to cut loose from time to time.' She added drily, 'Not often enough for Imogen's tastes though, if I'm any judge. If he marries her she'll give him no peace.'

Lisa said carefully, 'Then it isn't certain?'

Madalyn laughed. 'The only time anything can be taken as definite where Kyle is concerned is when he tells you. We share the same colouring, but that's as far as it goes.'

'You seem to get along well enough.'

'Oh, we do. That's because I don't stick my nose into his affairs and he leaves me to mine.'

Lisa smiled a little. 'The independent Hamiltons!'

'I suppose we are. He wouldn't thank me for shooting my mouth off the way I've just been doing, that's for sure!'

'He won't hear it from me.'

'I'm sure of that, too.' The other got nimbly to her feet. 'Once round the pool then we'll call it a day.'

For Lisa, Kyle's announcement over breakfast next morning that he was going across to St Thomas for a couple of days brought despondency in its wake, half anticipated though it had been. What Imogen wanted she obviously got, even where Kyle was concerned.

'He needs his head examining,' stated Madalyn disgustedly when he had departed. 'For once I might even break the rules and tell him so too, when he gets back!'

'Do you think it will do any good?' queried Lisa without expression, and received a wry glance.

'Doubtful. I just don't like to see him run when she calls. It isn't like him.'

'Perhaps he never felt as strongly about anyone before.'

'He'd have to be utterly besotted not to see what he's laying himself open to!' She moderated her tone to add, 'I've one or two things to see to this morning. Do you think you could amuse yourself for a couple of hours?'

'Of course.' Lisa gave her a bright smile. 'Don't worry about me.'

'Well, walk on up to the house with me, anyway,' with a glance towards the older woman silently contemplating the morning scene.

Following the glance, Lisa knew a sudden resolve. She had been here almost a week now and the situation had scarcely improved. Someone had to make the first move, and it obviously was not going to be her mother-in-law. 'I'll stay down here for a while,' she said. 'It's pleasant just sitting.'

Not for long, said the look on Madalyn's face, but she made no comment.

Broken only by bird calls, the silence stretched interminably after her departure. Lisa had to nerve herself to break it. 'I believe this was Paul's favourite place too,' she ventured.

For a moment there was animation in the older face, swiftly fading again. 'He liked to sit here and talk, yes.'

It was a start, if not much of one. Lisa seized the opening. 'Kyle said you were very close.'

Lack-lustre eyes turned her way briefly. 'Kyle never needed me the way Paul did. He never needed anybody. This Barrymore girl won't last.'

'You really don't think so?' Lisa was hard put to keep the eagerness from her voice. 'He certainly seems keen enough.'

'You'll see. She'll go the way of all the others.' Malice infiltrated her voice. 'You couldn't hold him either.'

She was getting mixed up in her mind, Lisa concluded. She said gently, 'I was married to Paul, not Kyle.'

'That didn't stop you. You wanted them both!'

Grey clouds swirled suddenly inside Lisa's head, making her feel sick and dizzy. 'That's ridiculous!' she heard her own voice protesting.

'Is it?' The other was watching her without sympathy. 'If you can't remember, how do you know?'

Gazing at her helplessly, Lisa was forced to concede that she had a point. It would certainly explain the way she felt about Kyle now; the way she had felt about him from the moment she had set eyes on him two short weeks ago. It might even explain Kyle's attitude towards her—his brother's wife who had set her cap at him too. No, it wasn't true. It couldn't be true!

'You can't run away from it,' Elaine Hamilton gibed as she made to rise. 'Not this time! If Kyle won't tell you the truth about yourself, then I'll do it for him.'

Lisa subsided again, fighting to regain her equilibrium. She was right. Running away wouldn't help anything. Whatever the truth, it had to be faced. 'So tell me,' she challenged.

It took the older woman a moment or two to gather her resources. When she did start to speak it was with bitterness. 'You never took me in, not from the start. I saw you for what you were. Oh, you'd got Paul twisted round your finger to start with, I'll grant you that, but he soon realised the mistake he'd made when you started making up to Kyle.'

'And what did he do about it?' Lisa forced the question through stiff lips.

'As far as he was concerned, Kyle could have had you for good.' She was warming to the theme now, her eyes alight. 'Only he didn't want you, so you tried to get Paul back.'

Lisa said softly, 'Was that why we went to St Thomas?'

'It might have been your idea; it can't have been his or you'd have been with him in the car instead of on a plane back to England. He must have told you right away that it was no use. Perhaps he only agreed to go to St Thomas in the first place so that he could put you on a plane home without any further trouble.'

There was every possibility that she had hit the nail on the head, thought Lisa numbly. Where Paul was concerned, at least. And Kyle? The images revolved: his face when he first saw her birthmark; the time down at the pool when she had imagined herself in his arms; the feeling whenever she was with him of being caught up in something she couldn't control.

'Surely if that had been the case he would have told you what his plans were,' she said, groping for some grain of reassurance.

'He would have told me after it was all over and done with, not before, in case it didn't work out the way he wanted,' came the answer.

'It's still pure supposition, though.'

'Of course it is. The only person left who knows the real truth is you.'

Lisa was white, unable to stop her limbs from trembling. 'Do you really think I could keep up a pretence of not remembering for this long?'

The reply came after a moment or two with reluctance. 'No, Kyle would have seen through you before this.'

'Then at least give me the benefit of the doubt before you condemn me completely.'

There was no softening of the older features. 'Why should I? My son died because of you!'

'I wasn't even there!' Lisa ran a distraught hand through her hair, wondering how she got through to the woman. 'It wasn't me in the car with him,' she added, immediately regretting the words because her mother-in-law had had enough to bear without being reminded of that fact.

'Just someone he offered a lift to after leaving you at the airport,' came the unmoved response.

'You mean the crash happened near the airport?'

For the first time Elaine Hamilton looked a little confused. 'It doesn't matter where it happened,' she said after a moment. 'He was just giving someone a lift, that's all.'

There was nothing to be gained, Lisa decided, from labouring the point. Whoever or whatever she might have been, Paul's companion in death was extraneous to the present conflict. She said softly, 'Do you still believe I sabotaged the car?'

Blue eyes flickered away. 'I was upset the day you arrived. Anyway, Kyle said it would have been impossible.' She made an abrupt movement. 'I don't want to talk about it any more. Why don't you leave me alone?'

Staying would be a waste of time, Lisa had to agree. How could she argue over something she knew nothing about? She needed to be alone herself to sort out her thoughts and emotions. Her and Kyle. If there was any truth at all in it, how far had it gone? Would he have been capable of taking advantage of the situation—or were those flashes of memory mere wishful thinking? The only way to find out was to ask him, and that she couldn't bring herself to do.

Kyle returned earlier than expected, and he returned alone. Imogen, he said in answer to his mother's enquiry, would not be joining them. He showed no inclination towards a more detailed explanation and she didn't pursue it, contenting herself with a meaningful glance in Lisa's direction. The latter refused to believe it could be quite that straightforward. Kyle looked like a man who had a problem to solve.

Imogen, it turned out, was not the only reason he had been to St Thomas. He dropped the bombshell later that evening after his mother had gone to her room.

'I think I know who the woman we buried was,' he said, pouring himself a second brandy.

Madalyn was the first to react. 'How?'

'Sifting evidence with the help of the police. Out of three possibles, there was one who got off a flight from Caracas that day but never reached home. Apparently, she'd told her husband she would be taking a taxi. From the timing, it seems there's a good possibility that Paul picked her up after dropping Lisa at the airport.' His glance shifted to his sister-in-law. 'Your name was on the passenger list for New York that day. Obviously there was never any cause to check it before.'

She said slowly, 'You're saying it could have been just a casual lift he was giving?'

'Doubtful. There would have been no reason for him to go through to arrivals unless he was meeting someone by prior arrangement.' The pause was timed. 'He'd just got back from Caracas himself that same morning.'

'Has the husband been informed?' asked Madalyn.

'Not yet. There'll have to be an exhumation and identification first—probably through dental or medical records. They'll be here tomorrow to take care of it.' The grey eyes sharpened as he saw Lisa's involuntary shiver. 'Are you feeling all right?'

She nodded, taking a firm grip on herself. 'I suppose you could say it was a goose walking over my grave. That poor man. What must he have gone through!'

Kyle inclined his head. 'In some ways it has to be a relief to him. Not knowing must be the worse part.'

Lisa could go along with that. Her own lack of knowledge was a constant torment. Looking at Kyle now, she felt the doubts flood back. If it was all true, surely there would have been some sign from him, some giveaway. Was it not possible that her mother-in-law had drawn faulty conclusions in the past? She had certainly been prejudiced enough.

'Did you use the *Seajade* to go across?' she asked without conscious intent, and gained some response in the faint narrowing of his eyes.

'No,' he said. 'I used the launch as usual.' There was a pause before he added evenly, 'As a matter of fact, I was thinking of taking her out tomorrow. Do either or both of you want to come?'

'Count me out,' said his sister promptly. 'I'm expecting a phone call from Tod. Do you good to have a blow though, Lisa.'

She found it difficult to hold Kyle's gaze, and impossible to resist the urge. 'Yes, I think it might. What time were you planning?'

'As soon as I've seen Scott—and providing there's nothing pressing, of course. Say around ten. We can eat lunch on board—make a day of it.'

Her limbs felt tingly, as if the blood flow had been temporarily suspended. 'That sounds fine, providing Madalyn doesn't mind being left on her own?'

The other girl laughed. 'I've been on my own before. Anyway,' with a sudden little gleam, 'I can always go over and get in Scott's hair. Just don't fall overboard!'

If Elaine Hamilton was right, thought Lisa numbly, the warning was too late. She had gone overboard a long time ago.

The matriarch of the family showed little reaction when advised of the proposed trip next morning. She seemed to have slipped back into apathy again.

'She doesn't want to get over Paul's death,' Kyle said bluntly on the way to the boat when Lisa expressed concern for his mother's state of mind. 'The medics call it melancholia. She seemed to snap out of it for a while when you came back, but obviously even that much effort is too much to sustain.'

'Wouldn't she be better away from the island and all the memories?' ventured Lisa.

'Perhaps. But she'd have to be taken by force, and I'm not prepared to inflict that on her.' He glanced her way as they came out from the cane on to the coastal road, tone altered. 'You look very nautical.'

Lisa looked down at her white drill slacks and rope-soled shoes, feeling the smooth, crisp cotton of the navy blue shirt against her skin. 'They were among my things,' she acknowledged. 'They seemed appropriate.'

'They are. We got the shoes in Roadtown.'

Her pulses jerked. 'You were with me when I bought them?'

'That's right.' He brought the jeep to a halt at the

roadside, switching off the engine and reaching for the hamper in the back.

She said softly, 'Did Paul like sailing?'

'No.' Kyle was sliding from his seat as he spoke. 'He preferred motor power.' He lifted an eyebrow when she continued to sit there. 'Having second thoughts?'

'Of course not.' She got hurriedly from the vehicle. 'If I could pick it up once I dare say I can do it again.'

'You don't need do anything today,' he assured her. 'She can be handled by one person. Just relax.'

She made herself smile. 'I'll try.'

There was no sense of *déjà vu* when Lisa stepped aboard the yacht, yet she found her body automatically adjusting its balance to take account of the gentle rocking movement. The *Seajade* was more spacious below than she had appeared from above decks, with a comfortable saloon and separate sleeping cabins.

'Take a look around and familiarise yourself while I get us under way,' Kyle invited, dumping the hamper in the well equipped galley. 'I'll show you how to use the stove, then you can make us some coffee.'

They left the jetty under motor power; Lisa could feel the throbbing of the engine under her feet as she moved through the craft. The teak panelling and dark blue fabrics throughout suggested practicality as the main aim. A boat built to be used, not kept as a showpiece. She guessed which was Kyle's own cabin because of the reefer-style jacket hanging on the back of the door. Well worn, she mused, fingering the material. Strange how men seemed to feel more at ease in old clothes, while women in general revelled in new.

She made an automatic grab as the garment suddenly came free of the door hook, catching it up before it hit the floor. The tab had given way, she saw. It must have been hanging by a thread. If Kyle had needle and cotton on board she could stitch it back on for him. That much she knew she could tackle.

Back in the saloon, she found a sewing kit in one of the lockers. Using heavy black thread, it took only a moment or two to stitch the tab back in place. Old or not, the garment was of obvious quality, with years of wear left in it. One of the navy blue buttons was coming loose too, she noted. She may as well do the job properly while she was about it.

She had the needle half-way through the first hole before awareness struck her. Heart thudding, she simply sat staring at it for several moments before reaching slowly for the sleeve. The left one had its full complement of three small buttons, the right one only two. There was no absolute certainty, of course. Not without actually comparing the one she had found with these. Yet there was no doubt in her mind that they were the same. Kyle had known where it was from—or at least, he had suspected. Secreted away in her writing case, a treasured memento of . . . what?

She returned the jacket to its hook behind the cabin door before getting down to making the coffee. They were under sail and running smoothly before the wind when she carried the two mugs carefully on deck. Kyle had taken off his shirt and was sitting bare-chested at the tiller, obviously enjoying the feel of the wind on his skin. He nodded an acknowledgement when she put the mug down beside him.

'Hope you brought a suit,' he said. 'I thought we might anchor off the cays and take a swim before we eat.'

'I'm wearing a bikini under these things,' Lisa admitted, trying to sound normal.

Kyle picked up the mug and took a drink, pulling an

appreciative face. 'You still make good coffee, at any rate. You surprised me with that the first time you came out.'

She said carefully, 'Meaning I'd given the impression of being unaccomplished in any direction up until that moment?'

His smile was dry. 'If that sounded like a chauvinistic remark, I apologise. You weren't an experienced sailor. I'd anticipated landlubber legs and a green face!'

'But you still let me come.'

'It was Madalyn's invitation that time.' He was looking ahead to the spit of land just showing above the swell, adjusting the rudder to bear further to port. 'We'll get right in the middle where it's smooth water.'

The spit of land grew, split, became not one but six or seven coral islets. Kyle threaded the *Seajade* between them with confidence, sailing over reefs teeming with life in the clear green water.

'They're too deep to explore properly without scuba gear,' he said when they were safely at anchor, 'but we can see enough to be going on with. You'd better use the ladder till you get your confidence back. You were only just learning to dive when you ...' his mouth compressed suddenly and fleetingly '... went away.'

And what else? she wondered painfully. A tremor ran through her as he stripped off his cotton jeans to reveal the brief black trunks—a quirk of memory, perhaps? Only when he had dived into the water did she move to take off her own clothing.

They stayed in the water for some twenty minutes or so just lazily splashing around. Kyle was first to suggest an adjournment for lunch, and was first up the ladder on to the deck, turning to offer her a casual hand before seizing the towels he had brought up ready from below and tossing her one across.

'Nothing like exercise for conjuring up an appetite,' he commented lightly. 'I'll fetch the food up here. It's too hot below.'

It was also too confining, Lisa reflected. She needed space between them—room to breathe.

He was back in short order bearing the hamper he had brought from the house. Inside lay a veritable feast of cold meats, newly baked crusty rolls, mouth-watering cheese-cake and fresh fruit. They ate picnic-fashion on the cabin roof, tossing the occasional titbit to the gulls and pelicans which inhabited the cays.

'Do you think it's true that Robert Louis Stevenson had the Virgin group in mind when he wrote *Treasure Island*?' Lisa asked, biting into a juicy nectarine.

'So it's said. They were a regular haunt for pirates, anyway.' Kyle was stretched out, hands clasped comfortably to support the back of his neck. 'That was before the planters arrived. The first Hamilton to land here helped establish law and order. In return he was granted sole rights to any one of the unoccupied islands. He named his choice after his wife.'

'There's never been any attempt made to take it back?'

'There might have been, except that he was obviously a wily old bird. He made sure the whole thing was put in writing. The deeds are lodged in a London vault. I checked on them myself this last visit.'

'But that wasn't your main reason for being in London?'

'No, I had business to take care of.' He was silent for a moment, eyes half closed against the sun's glare. 'Fate moves in strange ways.'

'Doesn't it?' She tried to say it as lightly as he had, but the words stuck in her throat. She knew an almost unbearable urge to reach out and lay her hand on the broad chest, to spread her fingers through the tangle of dark hair and feel the beat of his heart. It wouldn't be the first time, for certain. She had done that, and more. The moment was now; it wasn't going to get any easier. Finding the right opening was the hardest part.

'I stitched the tab back on your jacket,' she got out. 'The one hanging on the cabin door. There was . . . is a button missing from the sleeve.'

'I know.' He hadn't moved a muscle. 'The twin of the one you showed me the other night.'

'Or the same.' Lisa swallowed, taking her courage in both hands. 'Kyle, I have to know the truth—the whole truth. How did I come to have that button in the first place?'

'The question I've asked myself is why?' He was watching her with enigmatic eyes. 'You wore that jacket once.'

Her voice sounded thick in her ears. 'When?'

'The day we got caught in the squall.' The pause seemed to stretch for ever. 'The day we made love for the last time.'

CHAPTER SIX

SUSPICION was one thing, Lisa thought numbly, confirmation quite another. Several seconds elapsed before she could gather herself to speak, the shake in her voice no surprise. 'The *last* time?'

'That's right.' He had come up on an elbow, watching her dispassionately. 'I had to go away for a couple of days. The accident happened the day after I left.'

She said painfully, 'You didn't even trust me, Kyle. You told me that yourself.'

His smile was faint. 'Only initially, and it didn't stop me wanting you. I used to lie awake nights driving myself crazy imagining you and Paul together. When he began losing interest I stepped in. I'm not making excuses. There aren't any.'

Lisa gazed at him, her mind still refusing to accept what her body already knew was true. 'Those times you brought me out on *Seajade* . . .?'

'That's how it started. Just the two of us alone together. More than flesh and blood could stand!' The last with irony.

'How long was it going on for?'

'A couple of weeks at its peak. Madalyn was away, and Paul . . . well, he wasn't around all that much, anyway.'

Green eyes tried to penetrate grey, failing because he wasn't letting her in. She said thickly, 'You're making out it was all your fault. Your mother believes I made all the running.'

'When did she tell you that?'

'The morning you went to St Thomas. We had a long talk. She saw . . .'

'She saw what she wanted to see,' he interrupted hardily. 'Whatever you did it had to be wrong. I'm not trying to save you from anything, Lisa. You were vulnerable and I took advantage of it.'

'Just like that.'

'Not quite.' Voice and eyes were steady. 'I was in pretty deep by then. So much so I was ready to ignore the obvious difficulties. It was only when I found out you'd gone back to Paul that I realised I'd been living in a fool's paradise.'

Her throat hurt. 'You mean I'm not just an adultress, but there wasn't even any real feeling involved on my side?'

'Not quite true. It wasn't just a sexual affair. You were as drawn to me as I was to you.'

'Not enough, apparently, to stop me wanting Paul more.'

Kyle's lips twisted. 'So it seemed at the time. Yet within a few hours of leaving St Amelia you were on a plane home to England and he was driving off with another woman. Doesn't make any sense, does it?'

Lisa passed the back of a hand over her aching forehead. 'None of it makes any sense!'

'The only way it's ever likely to is for you to remember what happened. In the meantime, you're just going to have to take my word for it that what I've told you is the truth. I've no reason to lie about it.'

No reason at all, she acknowledged wryly. Fight against it though she might, from the very first moment of meeting there had been this awareness between them. She had lain in Kyle's arms, known the intimate intrusion of his body. That had to leave some impression, even if it was only on the subsconscious.

Her voice came low. 'You should have left me in ignorance that afternoon, we'd all have been better off.'

He shook his head. 'Even if I'd been capable of riding that kind of shock without opening my mouth, I could hardly have handled the situation any other way.'

'No, I suppose there would always have been the chance I might recover my memory involuntarily some time and appear out here demanding my rights.'

'Now you're putting words in my mouth.' His shoulders lifted in a wry shrug. 'All right, so I reacted badly to begin with. In a way, I suppose I was making you pay for what you did to me. I've been going through hell this last couple of weeks trying to sort myself out. One thing I do know,' he added with deliberation, 'whatever it was we had it's far from dead—for either of us. We've been given a new start, Lisa. Let's not waste it.'

She stared at him, heart thudding against her rib-cage. 'I don't . . .'

'You do. It's still there—everything we had together. You might have forgotten my face, but there's a part of you that responds to the same stimuli. We can build on that—starting right here and now.'

It was beyond her to put up any resistance as he took her face between his hands and kissed her. She felt the sudden melting sensation in the pit of her stomach, the flaring of an all too familiar heat through her veins as his tongue tasted the soft inner flesh of her mouth. Her mind went haywire—a jumble of fleeting, disconnected images gone before they were properly formed. It had been so long, so very long! She slid her arms up about his neck in order to get closer, wanting him, loving him, needing his strength. Nothing else mattered right now except being together.

Her bikini top came away in his hands, baring her

breasts to his touch. Her limbs turned to water at the exquisite sensations created by those long, clever fingers, her whole body filled with a delicious languor. Dreamily she allowed her hands to drift over hard muscle, to trace the tapering shape of him from shoulder down to waist and hip, remembering through her fingertips what her mind refused to release. Feeling, not thinking, that was the way.

It was Kyle himself who did the drawing back, though he didn't let her go. 'I want you,' he said thickly, 'but there are things we have to get straight first. You're going to marry me, Lisa.'

'You're Paul's brother!' The words were torn from her.

'That's inescapable fact, not unsurmountable. He's dead. There's nothing to stop us.'

'There's your mother—Madalyn.'

'They'll get over it. They'll have to.' His jaw firmed. 'I'm not giving you up again. Not this time.'

'Kyle, we can't,' she said, but there was no real conviction in the denial. She wanted him to persuade her that it was possible, to sweep away all her doubts. Kyle's wife. If only there was no one else involved!

'What about Imogen?' she asked desperately, searching his face. 'Only a week ago you wanted her here.'

'I invited her as a defence against you,' he said. 'For no other reason. I told her yesterday how things were.'

Green eyes darkened. 'All of it?'

'No. What happened in the past is between the two of us, no one else.' His thumb brushed her cheek, softly, tenderly, bringing a lump into her throat. 'I might never know what you really felt for me two years ago, and I'm not going to let it concern me. It's how you feel now that counts. Am I wrong in believing we share the same emotions?'

'No.' She said it with sudden flooding certainty, her smile

tremulous. 'I've been going through a kind of hell of my own this past two weeks trying to come to terms with what I did . . . do feel.'

Something in him seemed to relax. 'So that's it, then. The only question remaining is when?' He studied her, eyes reflective, seeing the return of doubt as her mind revolved. 'The easiest way—and perhaps even the kindest in the long run—will be to present my mother with a *fait accompli*. We can be in Roadtown in half an hour. I already have the licence.'

Lisa said blankly, 'Since when?'

'Two days ago before I took the shuttle across to St Thomas.' He smiled at her stunned expression. 'I was sure enough by then of what I wanted, and I don't intend taking no for an answer now either. All legal and above board this time—and the sooner the better. Why wait?'

Looking at him, she was seized by the sudden desperate urge to throw caution aside. She loved him now if she hadn't loved him then. As he said, why wait? Married to Kyle she could face anything, even the thought of never recovering her memory. She drew in a long, slow breath, closing her mind to everything but the moment.

'All right,' she said, 'let's do it.'

Afterwards, Lisa was to wonder how it was that Kyle had been able to command the services of a registrar at such short notice: for the present she was content simply to go along. The civil ceremony left little lasting impression. The only bit of it she remembered with any clarity was the moment when he slipped the newly procured gold band on to her finger, but even that failed to make it seem real. They were on their way back to the boat before the full impact hit her.

'I'm beginning to think we're both out of our minds,' she said shakily when they were on board. 'It's what everyone else is going to think!'

Kyle laughed. 'Let them. We knew what we were doing.' He drew her to him and kissed her, smiling at her response. 'You see? Made for each other!' His gaze kindled suddenly as he studied her face. 'Let's go below.'

'Not here.' Her skin felt flushed.

'Why not?' He sounded amused. 'We're on our honeymoon.'

'I wish we were,' she said impulsively. 'A real one, I mean. If we could just sail away somewhere until the whole thing blew over!'

'It has to be faced some time,' Kyle pointed out. 'Putting things off never helped. It isn't going to be easy, but we'll get through.' He kissed her again, lightly this time, then made a decisive gesture. 'So let's go and get it over with, then we can both relax.'

She said slowly, 'Does it have to be right away? Wouldn't it be better to wait a few days before we tell them?'

'What purpose would that serve?' Kyle was already on his way to start the engine. 'You're my wife and they have to accept it.'

'It's going to be such a shock,' she said. 'Particularly for your mother.'

'It will still be a shock a few days from now.' He turned his head to look at her, mouth slanted. 'Too late for regrets.'

'I don't regret it,' she denied, and wondered if that were strictly true. The reckless streak that had carried her through the last two hours was dissipating fast, leaving her deflated and uncertain. It was going to be so difficult facing her mother and sister-in-law. They could neither of them be expected to take the news in their stride. She dreaded the moment of confrontation.

They made a swift crossing, speaking little. Only when they were lying alongside the jetty back on St Amelia and ready to disembark did Kyle take her firmly by the arms and make her look at him.

'We made a decision,' he said, 'and acted on it. We have to take it from there. We're where we would have been two years ago if I'd only seen you first.'

Something inside her gave way. 'Do you really mean that?' she asked.

'Every word.' The grey eyes were intense. 'You're mine now, and you're staying mine. Paul is dead. He can't come between us any more.'

No one person can own another, she wanted to say, but she bit the words back. 'As far as I'm concerned, Paul never existed,' she said instead, softly. 'I love *you*, Kyle. I have since the first day we met—this time, at any rate.'

His face relaxed, the smile warm. 'That's all I need to hear. We're going to make a success of this marriage, Lisa. Between us we'll lay the foundations for a whole new line of Hamiltons.'

Children? She could scarcely think that far ahead. Her own smile was tremulous. 'Let's get used to being married first.'

He laughed. 'I didn't mean right this minute—although there's no harm in putting in a little practice.'

'No.' Lisa steeled herself against the desire to stay right here on the boat and forget what was to come. 'You were right the first time—the sooner we get it over with the better for all of us.' She hesitated before adding, 'When exactly are we going to tell them? Your mother won't be around when we get back to the house.'

'I'll do the telling privately where she's concerned,' he

said firmly. 'Give her a chance to adjust before she sees you.'

Relief washed over her. That sounded so much better than the scene she had envisaged. All she had to face now was Madalyn's reaction.

They found her down at the pool, Scott with her. The two of them looked as if they might have been undergoing some disagreement, thought Lisa, viewing the two carefully expressionless faces turned towards them as she and Kyle approached. She scarcely knew whether to be glad or sorry that Scott was here too.

'You certainly made a day of it,' commented Madalyn on a designedly light note. 'Where did you get to?'

'Roadtown,' her brother supplied. He nodded pleasantly to the other man. 'Glad you're here, Scott. You can help us celebrate.'

Madalyn's eyes went from his face to Lisa's, sharpening in the process. 'Celebrate what?'

Kyle slid an arm about Lisa's shoulders, drawing her closer to his side. His tone was as casual, she thought, as if he had been announcing some everyday occurrence. 'We were married just over an hour ago.'

Madalyn, Lisa realised in the following moments, had far more control over facial expression than did Scott; the latter's jaw quite literally dropped. He was, however, the first to find his voice, albeit with obvious reservations.

'Congratulations.'

'Thanks.' His employer's smile was dry, his eyes still on his sister. 'Don't you have anything to say?'

'Apart from calling you a bastard for not letting me in on it, you mean?' she came back gruffly. 'Why the secrecy, anyway? You're both adults. You couldn't have been stopped.'

'It was just simpler this way.' The arm about Lisa

tightened for a moment and then was removed. 'It think it calls for a drink all round. There should be some champagne in the cooler.'

'Obviously well planned,' commented his sister, still without expression. 'I thought better of you, Lisa.'

'I'm sorry.' She couldn't think of anything else to say.

'She couldn't tell you anything because she didn't know herself until a few hours ago,' said Kyle smoothly over a shoulder from the bar. 'You could say I talked her into it over lunch.'

'It was a very good lunch,' quipped Lisa in an attempt to add humour to the atmosphere.

'It must have been.' Madalyn made a sudden impatient gesture, getting to her feet and coming to offer an impulsive hug. 'I'm the one who should be saying sorry. Put it down to shock. I'm glad, of course, if it's what you both wanted.' Her eyes searched Lisa's face. 'I still don't understand why it had to be done in such a hurry.'

'Yes, you do.' Kyle carried a tray bearing brimming glasses. 'I didn't want Mother throwing any obstacles in the way.'

'She's going to react the same way whenever you tell her,' Madalyn responded, taking a glass from him. 'She can hardly be expected to like it.'

'Then she'll have to learn to bear it,' he said hardily. 'One way or another. It's time she started getting over Paul's death—time we all stopped pandering to her. It wasn't Lisa's fault that he died. She was gone when it happened.' He gave a glass to Scott and took the last one for himself, raising it with a satirical glint. 'I realise it isn't the done thing to drink a toast to oneself, so I'm doing it to the future. Life's a gamble all the way through. The best we can hope for is a chance.'

'Amen to that,' echoed Madalyn. She was looking at Scott, expression much the same as her brother's. 'Combined with a little faith and effort, when it comes.' She gulped once at the sparkling liquid, holding the glass between finger and thumb as her glance returned to her brother. 'Getting down to practicalities, where do we site the bridal suite?'

'My present room is more than adequate,' he responded easily. 'It just needs Lisa's things transferring.'

'I can do that myself,' she put in hastily. 'No need to trouble the staff.'

'They'll have to be put in the picture,' Madalyn pointed out. 'It's going to be the main topic of conversation for days to come, I hope you realise.'

'They'll soon find something else to talk about.' Kyle paused. 'Did Tod decide when he was arriving yet?'

'Yes.' Madalyn's face gave nothing away. 'Tomorrow. I'm not sure how long he'll be staying.' Her own pause was timed. 'I'm assuming you already told Imogen your plans?'

'Naturally.'

'I won't ask how she took it.'

'Might be as well,' Kyle agreed without inflection. 'Did the exhumation present any problems, Scott?'

'None they told me about,' came the steady reply. 'They said they'd be in touch when they had some definite news—maybe in a couple of days or so.'

Kyle shrugged. 'It's pretty much a foregone conclusion anyway. Not a job I'd relish myself.'

Nor she, thought Lisa, controlling a shudder. Sitting here now, she felt disorientated, like a fish out of water. In one short afternoon she had stepped from one role she didn't remember to another she couldn't take in. Kyle's wife. Was it really true? Surreptitiously she fingered the wide gold band, caught Madalyn's eye and abruptly desisted. It was true enough all right. No getting away from it. From here on in it was she and Kyle together, all the way through.

Scott declined Kyle's invitation to stay to dinner. He had, he said vaguely, a lot of things to catch up on. Madalyn made no attempt to accompany him to his car, murmuring a stony goodbye from where she sat.

'I suppose I'd better go and spread the news,' she said when he was out of sight. 'They can take care of the change-over while we have dinner. It shouldn't take all that long. Are you waiting till then to tell Mother?'

Kyle drained his glass and put it down. 'There's no time like the present.'

'Do you want me to come with you?' asked Lisa reluctantly as he got to his feet.

He shook his head. 'Better if I see her alone.' He gave her a reassuring smile. 'She'll probably not come down tonight.'

Lisa hoped not. By morning she might feel better equipped for the confrontation. Her nerves quivered at the thought of the night to come. If Kyle's mere touch could strike chords in her memory, perhaps in his arms the whole curtain would finally lift. At least there were no shocks in store for her now. She knew it all.

Despite her statement of intent, Madalyn made no immediate move to follow her brother. 'I think I may be missing a chapter or two of this saga myself,' she said after a moment or two. 'I was in Australia when the accident happened. I'd been there for several weeks. Am I wrong in imagining that this marriage of yours isn't perhaps as off-the-cuff as it might appear?'

'I'm not sure what that's supposed to mean,' Lisa returned steadily, and saw her sister-in-law smile.

'You know all right. There's been something between the two of you all along.' She held up a hand as Lisa made to speak again. 'I'm not criticising. Paul never deserved you anyway. I only hope you've done the right thing, that's all.'

'We love each other,' Lisa said softly. 'That's all we need.'

The smile took on a wry slant. 'It isn't always enough. Not for everyone. Is Kyle planning on getting away for a spell?'

Lisa shook her head. 'Not from what he said.'

'Then he should. You could take the *Seajade* and cruise down to Barbados, or wherever else the fancy takes you. Just spend some time alone together.'

'It sounds wonderful,' agreed Lisa wistfully. 'But I think he feels he's needed here.'

'Scott can cope. He can handle anything that doesn't involve any risk!' Grey eyes met green, lit by an emotion half-way between anger and despair. 'What do you do with a man who believes all women are the same under the skin?'

'I don't know,' Lisa admitted. 'Except try to prove him wrong.' She added slowly, 'Are you in love with Scott, Madalyn?'

The laugh jarred. 'We've been lovers for the last year, if that answers the question. And yes, I've slept with Tod too.' She made a sudden wry gesture. 'I'm sorry. That wasn't called for. Put it down to the old green-eyed monster, if you like. You and Kyle arrived at a bad moment. I'd been giving Scott an ultimatum—all or nothing, in effect.'

'And he chose nothing?'

'That's about the sum of it. He said he was leaving Tod a clear field.'

Lisa said hesitantly, 'Was inviting Tod such a good idea?'

'Of course it wasn't. Desperate measures aren't based on

good sense. I was using him, that's all, only it didn't work out the way I hoped. I don't suppose I merited a happy ending.'

'You don't feel anything for Tod?'

'Yes, I feel something. It just doesn't go as deep as it should.' She sighed suddenly. 'I'm going to have to tell him, aren't I?'

'It would seem fairer. Scott might see things in a different light if the competition is removed.'

'It isn't the competition that holds him back so much as the conviction that marriage ruins a good relationship. He says he's been through the mill once and he couldn't take it again.' Her tone briskened. 'Anyway, I shouldn't be burdening you with all this. Just forget about it, will you?'

'Kyle doesn't know?' Lisa ventured.

'No, he doesn't. And I don't want him to know. It's enough that I unloaded on you.' Madalyn rose, reaching for her wrap. 'I'll see you later.'

It was almost dark, the fireflies already dancing. Lisa sat for several minutes looking at the gently lapping water. She felt sympathy for Madalyn who couldn't have the man she loved, but she wished the other had kept her problems to herself. If marriage could ruin a good relationship, what were the chances for one as tenuous as hers and Kyle's? Love was only a part of it.

He was waiting for her in her bedroom when she went back to the house.

'I was just about to come looking for you,' he said. 'What kept you so long?'

'I was thinking,' Lisa acknowledged.

His brows lifted quizzically. 'With what conclusions?'

She forced a smile. 'I didn't say I was thinking straight.' Her eyes searched his. 'How did your mother take it?'

'Surprisingly well, considering. In a way, I think she'd rather think of you as my wife than Paul's widow.' He paused before adding dispassionately, 'She's talking of leaving St Amelia.'

Lisa said unhappily, 'Because I'm here?'

'Because the memories are. She has a sister in Washington. She wants to make a new start there. Not an impulsive decision. She says she's been doing a lot of thinking herself these last few days.'

'And you haven't tried to persuade her to change her mind?'

'No.' His gaze didn't flicker. 'We've never been all that close. She can always come back if she does change her mind, only I doubt she will. Even at the best of times she was never really happy here.'

'Do you think she might have been better off with Paul's father?'

Kyle shrugged. 'Apparently, he didn't want to know.'

Her eyes opened wide. 'She told you that herself?'

'When I was nineteen.' He shifted his weight from the window-sill where he had been leaning, tone dismissive. 'It was all a long time ago. I'm more concerned with now. Are you going to come over here to me or shall I come over there to you?'

Her voice came low. 'It's going to be dinner time soon.'

'Not that soon.' His voice roughened. 'What are you afraid of, Lisa?'

'Everything,' she admitted huskily. 'I'm not the same person you ... knew before.'

'Is that all?' He sounded almost relieved. 'You might have built up a new outer shell, but you're still the same underneath. Earlier, on the boat, it was as if the last two years never happened. You wanted me then.'

'I still do.' She was trembling but resolute. 'Just don't give me the option.'

Grey eyes flared with sudden passion. He reached her in a couple of strides, swinging her up in his arms to carry her across to the bed. Lisa reached for him hungrily, blocking out everything but the desire rising swift and sweet inside her. She was Kyle's wife now, not Paul's. The memories started here.

He undressed her slowly, tenderly, the touch of his hands and lips flaming her senses to unbearable proportions. She watched him slide out of his own clothing, relishing the breadth of his shoulders, the long, clean limbs, the hard-muscled belly and proud manhood. He was all male, this man of hers. And he was hers. She wore his ring. Remembering no longer mattered. Not now.

There was sensuality in the movement of her body beneath him when he came down over her. She ran light fingers over his back, holding him with the very tips of her nails as they merged together, eyes closed tight, lips forming sounds without shape or form, hips rising to a rhythm as old and as natural as the hills. It felt so good, so right, so utterly, wonderfully consummate. There had never been nor ever would be again a man like Kyle. She had always known that. Always, always, always . . .

He stayed with her afterwards, head pillowed on her shoulder, arms holding her close. In relaxation he was heavy, but she didn't care. She felt cherished, protected, totally content. When he slid over on to his side he took her with him, running possessive hands down her spinal column to cup the curve of her buttocks.

'Beautiful!' he murmured. 'Firm and rounded and utterly tantalising! I remember the first time I saw you in a bikini. I wanted you so much I had to get into the water to cool off!'

Lisa put her lips to his throat, tasting the faint tang of salt on his skin. 'Was I really so desirable?'

'Utterly.' He kissed her gently, inserting the tip of his tongue between her lips and smiling at the involuntary tremor. 'I tried keeping you at arm's length, but it was hard work when all I really wanted to do was make love.'

'Did Paul know how you felt?' she asked.

'Paul wasn't all that observant.'

'Especially over someone he didn't even care about.' Her voice was muffled.

Kyle's arms tightened a fraction, holding her closer. 'He cared in the beginning—as much as he was capable of. It wasn't his fault that his emotions didn't run very deep. Anyway, that's all in the past. We're only concerned with the future. Do you feel any better about things now?'

She laughed. 'Do you really need to ask?'

'I'm not talking about the physical side. How do you feel mentally?'

'Like a whole new woman,' she said. 'A complete one at last.' She added softly, 'I love you so much, Kyle.'

His eyes kindled again. 'Convince me some more.'

In his early forties, Tod Sherman was older than Lisa had anticipated. He was also the complete antithesis of Scott, a big, bluff Texan whose business empire stretched far beyond the confines of that state.

'I feel like Gulliver when I come down here,' he confessed to Lisa on the second morning of his visit, when the two of them had been left temporarily alone. 'My ranch back home is twice the size of this whole island!' He added with a grin, 'Not as pretty, maybe. Cattle need a lot of grass.'

Lisa smiled back. 'You run it yourself?'

'No way. Too many other commitments.' His tone altered. 'Madalyn told me about your little problem. That's real bad.'

'I've stopped thinking about it,' Lisa acknowledged truthfully.

'Best way. One of these mornings you're gonna wake up and it'll all be there.' There was another pause, another change of tone. 'You and she seem pretty close.'

'Fairly.' She was cautious, sensing what was coming.

'You think I'm too old for her?' asked Tod bluntly.

'Not necessarily.' Lisa was doing her best to be both fair and honest. 'Kyle is eleven years older than I am, if it comes to that.'

'I'm forty-three,' he admitted. 'That makes eighteen—leastways, it did when I was in school.'

Lisa could say it and mean it. 'You don't look it.'

'Thank you, ma'am,' he drawled. He shook his head, the smile fading. 'Doesn't much matter, does it? If she was as keen on the idea as I am I guess she'd have said yes before this.'

'Some women take a long time making up their minds.'

His sideways glance underlined the triteness of that comment in a way no words could have done. 'I've given myself this one week to make her mind up for her. After that it's curtains.'

'Try telling her that,' Lisa suggested, wishing he would leave her out of the affair. 'Perhaps an ultimatum is what she needs.'

'Maybe.' He sounded anything but convinced. 'I'd a suspicion she might be harbouring a soft spot for this manager of Kyle's. Spend much time round here, does he?'

'He doesn't have all that much spare time.' Lisa saw her

sister-in-law approaching with heartfelt relief. 'Here's Madalyn now.'

The latter was wearing jodhpurs and boots, unlike her guest, who looked thoroughly western in jeans and chequered shirt. 'Let's go,' she said briefly, and hesitated before adding to Lisa, 'Mother has something she'd like to say to you. Will you go up and see her?'

It was Lisa's turn to hesitate. In the last two days Elaine Hamilton had not addressed one single word to her, nor even acknowledged her presence. Whatever she had in mind now it was hardly likely to be an olive branch she was offering. She didn't want to see her. Not without Kyle's support. Only Kyle was out at the plant with Scott, and wouldn't be back before lunchtime.

'I'll go,' she agreed reluctantly. 'Enjoy your ride, both of you.'

It was the first time she had seen inside the door of her mother-in-law's room. Two knocked into one, she realised on entering in answer to the invitation. There was a pleasant sitting as well as a sleeping area, the whole decorated in apple-green and white. Mrs Hamilton was seated in a small armchair by one of the windows with what looked like a photograph album on her knee. The eyes she turned on Lisa were resolute.

'I'll be leaving tomorrow,' she said without preamble. 'My packing is almost done. You'll be able to move in here, you and Kyle.'

'We're comfortable enough where we are,' Lisa murmured, wondering what all this was leading up to. 'Anyway, you might want to come back.'

'I shan't be back,' came the decisive reply. 'I'm doing what I should have done years ago—what I would have done if it hadn't been for Paul. He needed me, you see.'

'I'm sure he did.' Lisa's tone was gentle. 'It's always said that a boy's love for his mother is something very special.'

'Some boys. Kyle never had any feeling.'

'You're wrong.' Lisa tried to say it with conviction. 'Perhaps you simply never gave him the chance to show it, that's all.'

'He's like his father was before him,' ignoring the last. 'All he really cares about is St Amelia. Not that it should bother you. You got what you wanted when he married you.'

'I love him,' Lisa stated with defiance. 'There was no calculation.'

'The same way you pretended to love Paul until he saw through you,' on a note of scorn. 'He made a mistake and paid for it with his life. Oh, I accept that you had nothing to do with the actual crash,' as Lisa opened her mouth to protest, 'but it was because of you that he was there that day at all. You lost your memory because there were things you didn't want to remember. At least it proves you had a conscience once.'

There was nothing Lisa could say to that. The theory was one already advanced to her by the psychiatrist she had been seeing in London. She had found it depressing enough then in its suggestion that no matter how much she told herself she wanted to recover her memory, her subconscious was fighting to keep it suppressed.

'I don't really think this is doing either of us any good,' she said, low-toned.

'You're wrong there. It's making me feel much better.' The faded blue eyes had a malicious glint. 'I hope you don't imagine Kyle married you for any other reason than to secure his holdings? He told me himself it was the only way he could be sure of retaining control. You deserve each other, the two of you. You might even manage to keep his interest for a little while, only sooner or later he's going to start looking round for some diversion, you mark my words.'

Lisa turned blindly away, unable to bear another minute. She felt sick inside. It wasn't true, she tried to tell herself. Kyle loved her the way she loved him. Yet, he had never actually said the words, had he? Actions might speak louder, but they could also convey the wrong message. For two days she had been living in a fool's paradise.

The house was stifling. She needed fresh air. Somehow she reached the hall, making for the front entrance to stand for a moment or two on the veranda drawing in deep breaths. One of the plantation jeeps was parked under the windows, ready for immediate use. Lisa hadn't attempted to drive since she had been here, but the desire to get away was stronger than doubt over her ability. Sliding behind the wheel, she turned the key in the ignition, hearing the engine fire through a kind of fog in her mind. She had done this so many times before: there was nothing to it. Gear lever into first, ease out on the clutch and she was moving smoothly forward, gravel crunching beneath the tyres. Head for the plant, she thought numbly. Make Kyle tell her the truth. Except that she didn't need to hear it from his lips because it was all coming back to her, the images tumbling over each other as the doors opened wide . . .

CHAPTER SEVEN

'I'M NERVOUS,' Lisa admitted as the plane began its descent. 'Supposing they don't like me?'

Paul laughed, devil-may-care blue eyes taking on an added glint. 'Like it or not, they can't do anything about it!'

It was hardly the kind of reassurance for which Lisa had been looking, but she already knew it was all she was likely to get. Looking out of the port at her side to the approaching island, she let her mind rove back over the past few weeks, wondering once again at the sheer fantasy of it all. Everything had happened so fast—like being on a helter-skelter with no way of pulling up and taking a long, hard look at the terrain ahead.

Aunt Susan's death had begun the sequence of events. The house where they had lived was mortgaged, which meant it had had to go. After all the bills were paid, the estate had realised a little over three thousand pounds. Enough to put by for a rainy day—or to take her on one grand, reckless splurge and provide memories to last her a lifetime. Winter sporting had always seemed to her the very essence of a holiday with a difference, and a few sessions on a dry ski slope had provided her with the rudiments. What she lacked in skill, her tutor had told her, she made up for in sheer nerve. Certainly she had known no fear of the swift downward swoop, only exhilaration.

Paul was the icing on the cake. He had picked her up on her second day out and they had been together since. His proposal had been the last thing she expected from a man of his kind, even if it was what she had secretly dreamed of.

There had been no opportunity to return to England before coming out here to the Caribbean, nor, if she were honest, did she regret that fact. She had no real home any more back there, no family, not even a close friend. There had never been time for any outside relationships. Not with an invalid aunt to look after. The pension that had kept them both going had died with the latter, of course, and she knew that without experience, she would have had trouble in finding a job. The knowledge that she need never worry about such things again still left her feeling bemused.

Touchdown brought her back to the present again with a jerk. This was only Tortola; they still had to get to St Amelia. Last night, in their hotel bedroom, she had been devastated to learn that Paul had not yet told his family that he was married. He had simply informed them that he was bringing someone with him, he admitted.

'It's a surprise,' he had said, smiling down into her eyes as he held her. 'You're the last thing they'll be expecting from the black sheep of the family.' The smile acquired a sudden edge. 'I'm not really a Hamilton, you see. My mother had an affair with another man. I was the result. I never knew my real father. He apparently took off like a rocket when he heard the news.'

Lisa reached up and laid her fingers softly against his lips, feeling for him in his bitterness. 'How did you find out?'

'I overheard my mother telling Kyle about it. I was twelve years old, but I understood what it meant.'

Kyle was Paul's older brother; Lisa already knew that much. Her brow wrinkled. 'Why would she tell him?'

'I'm not sure. It wasn't long after my . . . his father died. They were having some kind of disagreement. I think she might have said it just to shock him.'

'And was he shocked?'

The laugh was short. 'With Kyle, who'd know? As the eldest son he'd inherited outright anyway, so it didn't make any difference.'

Lisa said perplexedly, 'But I thought you said you were half-owner?'

'Only because Kyle made me a partner last year. Don't ask me why. I was as surprised as anybody.'

'Perhaps he wanted to make up to you for something that was no fault of yours,' Lisa suggested tentatively.

'Whatever, I'm not one to look a gift horse in the mouth.' Blue eyes glinted as they studied her face on the pillow. 'Would you still have married me if I'd been a poor man?'

'Not a chance,' she responded, not taking the question seriously. 'After all, what other attraction could you possibly have?'

'I'll show you,' he said, seeking her lips. 'Prepare to be ravished, wife!'

It was the right word, Lisa thought now, fumbling for the catch of her seat-belt as the plane came to a final halt after taxiing clear of the runway. Paul made love with verve and passion but little tenderness, leaving her aching in more than the one sense. She tried not to let that lack worry her too much. Love had to grow and develop between two people; it was rarely perfect from the start. According to what she had read, one was supposed to discuss one's needs with one's partner, only she found it impossible to tell Paul that he wasn't making her totally happy, especially after one bare week of marriage. There was more to the latter state than lovemaking, anyway. Once she got over the trauma of meeting her new family there would be time and to spare for learning each other's ways. If only he had told them about her!

Tortola's airport was situated on a smaller island off the eastern tip, the two connected by a bridge. They took a taxi

down to the wharf to find the launch already awaiting their
arrival. Temporary reprieve or no, Lisa was thankful to
find that none of the family had elected to come and meet
them.

'Seems you're going to be first to hear the news, Josh,'
said Paul cheerfully to the tall young West Indian who had
brought the boat across. 'Meet the new Mrs Hamilton.'

A wide grin broke across the dark face. 'You done it this
time, Mr Paul!'

'All the way.' He took Lisa's hand, raising it laughingly
to his lips. 'Don't look so worried, sweetheart. They're
going to love you!'

She could only hope so. The closer she got to her new
home the worse she felt. The one small shred of comfort was
in the thought that Paul's sister, Madalyn, was only a
couple of years or so older than herself. That surely had to
give them something in common.

St Amelia was everything she had imagined: edged with
shimmering white beaches and waving palms, teeming
with bird life, with colour. Even the cane was picturesque,
greeny yellow stalks lofting skywards in every direction. At
any other time Lisa would have revelled in the scenery.
Right now she could summon no more than a passing
interest. Paul himself seemed oblivious to any vibes from
her direction, a tuneless little whistle on his lips as they
drove. He had been away for three months, she knew, yet it
might have been only a few days for all the attention he
paid to the growing crop. Kyle and his manager ran the
plantation between them; she knew that, too. Paul, to put it
in his own words, was a sleeping partner. For the first time
it occurred to her to wonder if that had been Kyle's
intention when he had handed over half the estate to his
younger brother. Not that it made any difference to the
way she felt about the latter, of course, she told herself in

swift loyalty. She had fallen in love with the man he was, not the one he perhaps should have been.

Her first glimpse of the house was a comfort of sorts. It looked like a home, solid and gracious and somehow dependable. Paul had expressed surprise when she asked where they would live. Tamarind was big enough for all of them, he had said. It would be quite ridiculous to consider building another house just for two. It had been a little too soon to mention the probability of their being three, or even more, in time to come. Lisa wasn't even sure how she felt about having children herself yet. She was only twenty. There was plenty of time.

The young woman with mid-length dark hair who was descending the staircase as they entered the house looked nothing like the man at Lisa's side. Her features were striking rather than merely pretty, her eyes a fine grey. Her smile when she saw the two of them was just a shade restrained.

'Good to have you back, Paul,' she said. 'I've just been checking on your guest's room,' directing the smile in Lisa's direction. 'Hello, there. Sorry I don't have your name. This brother of mine doesn't believe in wasting words when he sends a telegram. Anyway, you're very welcome.'

'Her name is Lisa.' Paul was grinning, obviously enjoying himself. 'Where's Mother, and Kyle?'

'Mother's down at the garden house, Kyle's eating at Scott's place.'

'Damn!' for a moment he looked crestfallen. 'I wanted you all together.'

Grey eyes went from one to the other, registering Lisa's discomfiture. 'For what?'

'To make the announcement.' He shrugged dismissively. 'Oh, well, it isn't that important. Lisa and I were married a week ago, so we shan't be needing that guest-room after all.'

Watching the sudden leap of expression across the other girl's face, Lisa could only sympathise. Paul wasn't stuck for a turn of phrase; he could have found some better way of imparting the news. It was as if he had wanted to shock.

'I'm sorry to spring it on you this way,' she said awkwardly. 'I—It all happened rather fast.'

'So it seems.' Madalyn made an admirable effort. 'Well, congratulations.'

'Thanks.' Paul leaned forward as if on impulse and kissed his sister lightly on the cheek. 'I knew I could rely on you to take it in your stride!'

Madalyn's laugh was short. 'I could always count on you for surprises!' She met Lisa's troubled gaze and softened her tone. 'You must be longing to freshen up after the journey. Why don't you go and break the news to Mother, Paul, while I show Lisa where her . . . your room is? I'll bring her along in a few minutes.'

'OK.' He sounded relatively unconcerned, his smile ignoring Lisa's swift glance of appeal. 'See you in a little while, then.'

Josh had brought in the luggage, features impassive as he looked to Madalyn for instructions. She made a decisive gesture. 'Bring them up to Mr Paul's room for now, Josh.' To Lisa she added, 'If you'd like to come on up?'

Josh went on ahead with Lisa's two suitcases, leaving the two huge ones belonging to Paul for another journey. Moving with speed and agility, he had deposited his load and was on his way back again by the time the two girls reached the head of the stairs. Madalyn led the way along the left-hand gallery to the door he had left ajar, standing back to allow Lisa prior entry. The room beyond was dominated by the four-poster bed with its carved posts and canopy of dark blue damask. Matching side curtains, at present tied back, were complemented by the paler blue of

the carpet and window curtains, the whole relieved by
plain white walls and a variety of artwork.

'The bathroom is through there,' indicated Madalyn,
pointing to a door on the far side. 'Take your time, there's
no rush. I'll wait for you.'

The walls within were lined with mirror glass. Washing
her hands at the inset bowl, Lisa met her own rueful eyes
and wondered what she was going to say to the girl outside.
Her sister-in-law, that's who she was. She wished suddenly
that she really was here just as a guest—or at least, as Paul's
fiancée. Anything rather than this situation. Madalyn, she
fancied, was going to prove the easiest hurdle to cross.

She was outwardly composed by the time she returned to
the bedroom. Enough so to meet Madalyn's gaze with
equanimity.

'It must have been quite a shock for you,' she said.

'It will have been even more of one for my mother,' came
the dry reply. 'Where did the two of you meet?'

'Switzerland,' Lisa acknowledged. 'On a skiing holiday.'

The other's sudden grin was appealing. 'Was it as
romantic as it sounds?'

Lisa smiled back, feeling herself relax a little. 'You could
say I was literally swept off my feet!'

'That sounds like Paul.' Madalyn paused. 'Did you let
your own people know yet?'

'I don't have any family—not that I'm aware of,
anyway.' Lisa kept her tone matter of fact. 'The aunt who
brought me up died a little while ago.'

'Poor you.' The sympathy sounded genuine. 'Well,
you've got one now. Whether you're going to think that a
good thing or a bad remains to be seen.' She pushed herself
upright from the window seat. 'Let's go get it over with.'

'Will it be that bad?' asked Lisa doubtfully, following her
from the room.

'Depends how Paul handled it,' came the reply. 'Mother hasn't seen him for three months. Sharing him with a wife isn't going to come easy.'

'I don't want to come between them in any way.'

Grey eyes slanted a glance. 'Of course you do. No wife would want to take second place in her husband's affections. Paul has to live his own life. She has to accept that.'

Lisa said softly, 'She still has you and Kyle.'

'Hardly the same, as you'll soon discover.' There was no particular censure in Madalyn's tone. 'Paul was always the apple of her eye.'

Because she had loved his father more than she had loved her husband? wondered Lisa fleetingly. That would explain a lot.

The gardens to the rear of the house took her breath away. She could be so happy in a place like this, she thought, sniffing pleasurably at the scent-laden air. Who wouldn't? So different from the neat little detached and pocket-handkerchief-sized garden where she had spent so many years. She could scarcely remember what came before that, but her parents had not been rich people either. The skiing holiday and Paul had opened her eyes to how the other half lived. It would even be true to say they had given her a taste for it. Fortune had smiled on her in every sense these last few weeks. She could only hope it would continue to do so.

Paul and his mother were seated by the poolside. The former looked relieved to see them appear through the shrubbery.

'Here she is!' he said. 'Come and say hello to Mother, Lisa. She's anxious to meet you.'

The older woman looked anything but, Lisa thought privately, summoning a smile as she met the cold blue eyes.

'How are you?' she asked tentatively.

'Paul tells me you're an orphan,' Elaine Hamilton retorted, ignoring the greeting.

'I suppose I am.' Lisa tried to make light of the moment. 'Although I never really felt one.'

'Who exactly were your people?'

Lisa's chin lifted a fraction. 'My father was a university lecturer. He and my mother were killed in a plane crash coming back from America when I was four years old. An aunt brought me up until she became ill. Then I looked after her.'

'Very commendable.' The pause was brief, the ice no nearer melting. 'I'm not going to pretend to be overjoyed because my son rushes into a marriage he can't possibly have considered, but as it's done I suppose we have to make the best of it. Madalyn, what's keeping lunch?'

'It's on its way.' From her tone, the other was as nonplussed by her mother's sudden switch as Lisa herself. 'Paul, you'd better open some wine in lieu of champagne.'

Lisa let out her pent breath on a small sigh. It could have been worse, she supposed, although not a lot. She felt dismissed as unworthy of further discussion—Paul's unfortunate mistake which had to be borne. She knew in that moment that her mother-in-law would never be her friend. At best she would be tolerated. It was a depressing outlook for the future.

Paul himself seemed unperturbed by the implication. At times during the meal, Lisa found herself wondering if he even recognised the lack of true acceptance in his mother's attitude. Here on the island, he apeared somehow different from the man she had hitherto known—or was it simply that he wasn't paying her the same amount of attention now as before? If his mother had to learn to share then so did she.

It was left to Madalyn to draw the newcomer to the family into conversation, Lisa was grateful for the consideration, hurt despite herself by Paul's lack of that quality. It was almost as if, having sprung his surprise, he had lost interest in the whole subject. Certainly he in no way gave the impression of being the loving bridegroom.

Elaine Hamilton's departure for what Madalyn explained was her regular afternoon siesta brought some improvement in atmosphere.

'You two pop off and get yourselves settled in,' she urged. 'There should be plenty of wardrobe space for you both—unless you have a lot more stuff to come?' The last to Lisa.

'Just a few things I put into storage when I had to leave my aunt's house,' Lisa admitted. 'I can send for them later.'

'What were you planning on doing with your life if you hadn't met Paul?' asked Madalyn curiously.

'Does it matter?' Her brother's voice held a note of impatience. 'She's here now, that's all that counts.'

Lisa hoped he meant that. She was beginning to have serious doubts.

They were doubts dispelled to a certain extent in the privacy of their bedroom, if not wholly. 'One of the compensations,' he said with some satisfaction in the quiet aftermath of their lovemaking. 'You'll have to learn to let yourself go a bit more, though,' he added carelessly. 'I could feel you holding back.'

Not holding back, just in need of more time, she wanted to say, but the words wouldn't come. 'I'm afraid your mother doesn't think I'm good enough for you,' she said instead.

Paul laughed. 'She wouldn't think any girl good enough for me! Don't worry, she'll get over it. Always providing you make me happy, of course.'

'Oh, of course!' She strove to keep her tone as

inconsequential as his. 'It's a wife's duty, isn't it?'

'Right on, babe!' He kissed the end of her nose, then rolled away from her to sit up. 'I'm going to take a ride. Coming?'

'I don't ride,' she said. 'Anyway, I still have to unpack.'

'Bella will do that for you.'

Lisa said quickly. 'I'd rather do my own.'

'OK, so do mine too while you're at it.' He was already on his way to the bathroom. 'I'll be gone a couple of hours.'

By four o'clock the unpacking was finished, those things in need of laundering neatly folded into the linen basket in the bathroom. One of the great delights in living in a house with servants had to be the lack of mundane household chores like washing and ironing, Lisa reflected, putting on the lid. She had done her share during her short lifetime. Aunt Susan had been a regular martinet when it came to keeping a clean and tidy home. It was going to seem strange at first not having to think of such matters, but it was a lifestyle one could easily adapt to, she was sure. There would be time to indulge in all kinds of new experiences. Riding, for instance. She had never even been on a horse. The yacht they had seen on landing belonged to Kyle, Paul had said. He himself preferred motor power—the faster the better. Recalling the long, graceful lines of the *Seajade*, Lisa wondered now if her brother-in-law might be prevailed upon to take her out in it. There was something about the sea that fascinated her; it always had.

At four-thirty, dressed in a simple apricot cotton dress she hoped might be acceptable by Mrs Hamilton's standards for late afternoon, she descended the stairs to find the house quiet and apparently deserted. Opening and closing doors quietly, and feeling like an interloper, she finally located the living-room, looking with delight at the white baby grand piano over by the window. Here was something she could do! If only she dared sit down and play on such an instrument. Yet why not? This was now her home. She could hardly go through the rest of her days waiting for permission to feel at ease.

She closed the double doors again before coming back to lift the keyboard lid and take her seat. The first tentative touch produced a sound so mellow that she shivered with pleasure. When she began to play it was without thought for anything but the music springing from her fingertips. As always, she felt soothed by it, taken out of herself.

It was some untold time later that she became aware of someone leaning against the jamb of the half-opened door, causing her to break off in mid-flow. There was enough likeness to Madalyn in the man's lean, intelligent features to make his identity obvious at once. Meeting the steady grey gaze, Lisa felt her stomach muscles tauten, her pulses accelerate. She couldn't think of one solitary word to say.

Kyle took the initiative out of her hands, his expression speculative. 'You must be Paul's guest. Don't stop. I was enjoying the performance.'

'I didn't realise you were there,' she said haltingly. 'You haven't . . . seen Paul yet?'

Dark brows rose a fraction. 'I only just got in. Was there any special reason why I should?'

'Yes. At least . . .' Lisa paused, biting her lip, realising it had to be up to her to put the record straight. 'I'm not Paul's guest,' she added with diffidence. 'I'm his wife.'

It was difficult to tell in the moments following that statement exactly what Kyle's reaction might be. He just stood there looking at her with narrowed eyes. When he did speak it was with an icy calm. 'When did *that* happen?'

'A week ago,' she returned unhappily. 'I—It was to be a surprise.'

'It's certainly all of that.' He was angry, she could see that now, but holding it in check. 'How old are you?' he demanded.

Twin spots of colour stained her cheeks. 'Old enough. And if the next question is going to be *who* am I, don't bother. Your mother already asked it.'

'Hardly surprising.' He came further into the room, closing the door behind him and standing with his back to it. 'I suppose this couldn't be some kind of joke you cooked up between you?'

'No, it isn't.' It was, Lisa thought wryly, anything but! 'I can show you our marriage certificate if you like,' she tagged on. 'It's all legal and above board.'

'I'm sure.' The strong mouth had thinned. 'Where is he?'

'Out riding,' she said. 'I'd have gone with him, except that I don't . . . ride, I mean. I'd love to learn, though. I just never had the opportunity before this.' She was prattling and she knew it, but she couldn't seem to stop. 'St Amelia is just as I imagined it would be. I can't think how Paul could bring himself to stay away so long!'

'Can't you?' The tone was dry. 'Which one of you was it wanted to come back?'

'Well, Paul, of course.' She was nonplussed by the question. 'Naturally, I wanted to meet his family too.'

'Oh, naturally.' The pause was timed. 'Tell me, how long had you two known each other before you . . . decided to get married?'

Lisa flushed, sensing what must come. 'About ten days.'

'Ten days,' he repeated. 'And you consider that long enough to find out all you need to know about a person?'

'No,' she acknowledged with a show of spirit. 'But then it's often said that it's impossible to know anyone properly without living with them first."

His lip curled. 'Only you had to have it legal and above board, of course.'

'It was what we both wanted.' Her cheeks had flamed again, with anger this time. 'I didn't trick or trap your brother into marrying me. I never even expected him to ask me!'

'I'll hold judgement on that score until I've talked with Paul,' came the cool response. 'In the meantime, I hardly need tell you to make yourself at home. You seem to have done that already.'

Lisa stayed frozen until the door had closed again behind the tall, clean-limbed figure, feeling the trembling start deep down inside as reaction set in. The man was hateful. Utterly hateful! The fact that he bore no physical resemblance to his mother meant little. He was her male counterpart in sheer disregard for other people's feelings.

In all fairness, came the small still voice of reason, there was some mitigation to be found in the fact that he had, so to speak, been dropped on from a height. All the same, he could have given her the benefit of the doubt until he had talked with his brother and learned the truth of the matter. As if she, or anyone else for that matter, could possibly orchestrate a marriage proposal! That was giving her credit for far more power than she was ever likely to possess.

How long she sat there miserably contemplating the immediate future she couldn't have said. When she did eventually stir herself into movement it was with extreme reluctance, and only because she could hardly continue to skulk in here for the rest of the day. By the time she came into contact with the rest of the family again she had to be in complete control of her emotions and able to ride any further innuendo, should it prove forthcoming. With Paul there to back her up all should be, if not exactly well, at least better. It could scarcely be worse!

The sun was touching the horizon before Paul put in an

appearance. He looked sulky, was her first impression—
like a small boy recently denied his own way.

'What the devil have you been saying to Kyle?' he
demanded without preamble. 'He just made me feel a
complete idiot!'

'He made me feel worse than that,' Lisa replied quietly. 'I
hope you told him it wasn't the way he seems to think.'

The blue eyes were suddenly evasive. 'I told him I was of
an age to marry whom I liked when I liked. Anyway,
there's nothing he can do about it.'

Except make my life a total misery, she thought numbly.
Paul was going to be little help, that was already obvious.
He had made his gesture, the rest was up to her. The scales
were falling from her eyes with a vengeance. Paul didn't
love her. At least, not in the way she had imagined. He had
married her on a whim and he was probably even now
beginning to regret it. The fact that he wouldn't, or
couldn't, quite meet her eyes seemed to bear out that
theory.

She made a valiant effort to regain some sense of
proportion. The time to start despairing was surely not yet.
Give it a chance; give them all a chance. In a little while she
would be able to look back on this raw beginning and laugh
at her fears.

CHAPTER EIGHT

HAD it not been for Madalyn during those first weeks, Lisa was convinced she would not have stuck it out. Having a mother-in-law who treated her with icy disdain and a brother-in-law who avoided speaking to her at all unless forced scarcely made for a comfortable existence.

'It's Paul Kyle's really up to here with,' Madalyn advised one afternoon when the two of them were alone together. 'He made him a partner in the hope that he'd take an interest in the plantation. Instead of which he's actually taken less. Where is he now, by the way?'

'He took the launch across to Roadtown,' Lisa acknowledged, and received an oblique glance.

'Didn't you want to go with him?'

'I wasn't asked.'

'Oh?' Madalyn sounded curious. 'You don't have to wait for an invitation from your husband, do you?'

Lisa lifted her shoulders in a shrug meant to be casual. 'I think he wanted to be alone for a while.'

'In Roadtown?'

'All right then, it was me he wanted to get away from.' Her laugh was brittle. 'Me, and all reminders of the mistake he made!'

They were reclining on loungers beside the pool. Madalyn came up on an elbow to view her. 'Aren't you being a bit premature?'

Lisa made a rueful little gesture. 'Probably.'

'Paul was always bored here,' said his sister flatly. 'You'd be better leaving the island altogether and making a home somewhere else.'

'It's such a lovely place,' Lisa murmured on a wistful note. 'He might not be bored if he'd do as Kyle wants and involve himself in the business—although I suppose he isn't really needed any more since you brought in a manager?'

'Since Kyle brought in a manager. I don't have anything to do with running the plantation, only the house. I dare say they could still find him plenty to do, only I can't see it coming off now.'

Lisa said slowly, 'But Kyle can surely insist on him doing something!'

'How? Having legalised the position, he can hardly rescind. Anyway, I doubt if he'd do it even if he could. Kyle stands by his mistakes.'

'I shouldn't have thought,' Lisa responded, 'that he made very many.'

Madalyn's smile was sympathetic. 'He's been a bit of a boor where you're concerned, hasn't he?'

'I suppose,' Lisa acknowledged with wry intonation, 'he still believes I tricked Paul into marrying me—although I don't know what lure he thinks I used!'

'Did you ever look in a mirror?' came the ironic comment. 'Not that I'm agreeing with him, mind, but don't underestimate your own attractions. It's all very well the pundits saying that looks aren't everything. In my experience, if you don't have them you don't even get to first base with the majority of men. If the stubborn idiot would only let himself get to know you he'd find out how wrong he is about you.'

'Thanks.' Lisa's heart warmed to the other girl.

'Let's go riding,' suggested Madalyn a moment or two later. 'Your muscles could still do with a little hardening off.'

'I don't like to keep borrowing your things,' Lisa confessed. 'Couldn't I just wear jeans?'

'Not unless you want your legs chafing. If it bothers you

that much we'll nip across to St Thomas and get you fixed up. It's been ages since I went on a shopping spree myself.'

Why not? Lisa reflected, feeling a stirring of interest. She had money of her own left. Somewhere at the back of her mind was the thought that perhaps she should leave what she had where it was in case of eventual need, but she pushed it away. They needed time, that was all. Time to adjust, time to grow together. They couldn't be the only ones to find the first few weeks, or even months, of living together difficult.

From the first tentative approach, she had taken to riding like a duck takes to water. Tamarind ran a stable of two, both Palomino geldings. Seated astride the English saddle as they cantered across open country, Lisa knew exhilaration. The sky overhead was a vivid blue, the sun's heat tempered by the ever-present trade winds to a caressing warmth on her bare arms. The short-sleeved white shirt she wore was one of her own, unlike the jodhpurs and boots which Madalyn had provided. Proficient though she was becoming at the art, she had not yet ridden with Paul, preferring, as she told Madalyn, to be capable of keeping up with anything he could do before attempting it. Paul was impatient with beginners. Had she shown any sign of nerves on the ski slopes she doubted if their relationship would have progressed beyond the first couple of days. Once or twice she had found herself thinking that it might have been better had she not been quite so daring—except that she would then probably never have known this part of the world. If only she could recapture that wonderful state of euphoria when Paul had suggested they get married, that initial certainty of feeling. Romance lasted so little time.

They had ridden in a north-westerly direction, cutting across the island. Breasting a rise, Lisa found herself looking down on the spreading roofs of the company warehouses,

with the tall chimney of the distillery itself an obvious
landmark. Beyond lay the protected harbour which housed
the loading dock. There was a ship in now, her hold open to
the swivelling crane.

'I thought we'd pay a call while we're in the area,' said
Madalyn blithely. 'Perhaps wangle ourselves some tea, if
we're lucky. Both Kyle and Scott were going to be at the
plant this afternoon.'

'Aren't they likely to be busy?' asked Lisa with reticence.

Madalyn laughed. 'This is a British island. Everything
stops for tea!' She urged her mount forward. 'Come on.'

It took them a few minutes to ride down into the enclave.
There was a lot of activity, with trucks coming and going,
though rather less noise than Lisa had anticipated. The
sickly sweet odour of molasses wrinkled her nostrils.

'You get used to it after a while,' Madalyn advised,
grinning at her expression. 'If you work with it all day you
don't even notice it. You'll have to get Kyle to give you the
conducted tour.'

Not unless he offered, came the thought. She would ask
Kyle for nothing. She hated the idea of bursting in
unannounced this way but, short of refusing to go along,
there was little enough she could do about it. He was
Madalyn's brother, after all.

They left the horses tethered to a fence outside the
distillery, making their way through the unloading bay
and up a flight of iron stairs to find both men together in the
small office.

'Surprise!' Madalyn announced cheerfully, pausing in
the doorway. 'We're both dying of thirst and not prepared
to be moved until it's been slaked!'

'In that case,' said her brother drily, 'you'd better both
come on in and find a seat before you collapse.'

'Tea's on its way,' said Scott, offering his own chair to
Lisa with a smile. 'We saw you coming from the window.

You look as though you'd been riding all your life!'

'It's coming along,' she acknowledged, smiling back at him. 'At least, I haven't fallen off yet.'

'You're not a rider until you have—and got back on again.' Kyle's tone was light. 'What brought you out this way?'

'A yearning for company,' chimed in Madalyn promptly. 'Paul went across to Roadtown.'

Kyle's eyes sought Lisa's, brows lifting. 'You didn't feel like making the trip?'

'No.' She avoided Madalyn's swift glance. 'I hope we're not disrupting your work schedule.'

'We finished for the day. As a matter of fact, we were just thinking of leaving.'

'Lucky we got here in time, then,' retorted his sister with bland intonation. 'You haven't been over to the house for ages, Scott. The invitation was an open one, you know.'

'I don't like to intrude.' The manager's pleasant features had acquired a sudden shuttered look.

'You don't have to worry about that. You're one of the family now. What about tonight?' She laughed. 'You can hardly plead a previous engagement!'

His smile seemed almost against his will. 'That's true.'

'That's settled, then.' Madalyn's eyes were bright. 'And afterwards Kyle can take us all out in *Seajade* for a couple of hours. I love sailing by moonlight!'

'You're too fond of organising people,' responded her brother, but he sounded amenable enough. 'How about it, Scott?'

'Sounds a good way of spending an evening,' agreed the other. 'Thanks.'

'It's doubtful if we'll get Paul to come,' said Madalyn to Lisa as the tea arrived. 'He hates sailing at any time. Did you ever do any yourself?'

Lisa shook her head. 'Perhaps I should give it a miss this

time,' she ventured. 'I might spoil it for everybody.'

It was Kyle himself who answered. 'We can always toss you overboard.' The grey eyes were faintly mocking. 'Like Jonah, except that there aren't any whales around St Amelia.'

'If there were they'd probably spit me right out again,' she came back, and saw a sudden spark light his gaze. As always when she looked at him, she could feel the tiny hairs prickling along her arms, the tensing of nerve and sinew. Not fear exactly, but close to it. She wasn't sure just what it was she was afraid of. She wasn't sure she even wanted to know.

'She'll be fine,' said Madalyn, breaking the momentary suspension. 'You'll have her crewing for you before you know where you are, Kyle. She picks things up very quickly.'

'That'll be the day,' he returned ambiguously. 'Are you going to pour this tea or leave it to stew?'

They left the plant together, all four of them, the men to their respective vehicles, the two girls as they had arrived.

'We'll eat early,' Madalyn told them before parting. 'Sevenish, say. Give us more time afterwards.'

'That nailed him,' she added with satisfaction when they were riding away. 'He spends too much time on his own, does that man.'

Lisa gave her an oblique glance. 'Are you attracted to him?'

'He intrigues me,' the other confessed. 'He's only Kyle's age, yet he doesn't seem to have any interest in enjoying life. Can you imagine any man being content with what Scott has here? In three months he's been to Roadtown just once!'

'Perhaps he just enjoys his work,' suggested Lisa mildly. 'Some men seem to put that above everything else.'

'If you're talking about Kyle, you're not entirely right.

He might work hard while he's at it, but he takes time off for other things.'

'Female company, you mean?'

'That's one of them.' Madalyn's glance was amused. 'You didn't imagine he was otherwise inclined, did you?'

Lisa thought of the strong, lean features, the muscular body, the sheer uncompromising masculinity of the man, shaking her head with a smile. 'Hardly. I just wondered why he hasn't found himself a wife yet, that's all.'

'Probably because he's still looking for a woman suited to the kind of lifestyle he leads himself. There can't be all that many willing to incarcerate themselves on an island the size of St Amelia for weeks at a time.'

'But it's so beautiful here,' Lisa protested. 'You do it.'

'I was born here and I love it. All the same, I like getting away from time to time.' There was a pause before she added, 'As a matter of fact, I'm off to Australia next month. We have some distant relatives out there—including several cousins around my age. It's been arranged for ages.'

Lisa strove to conceal the desolation engendered by the news. 'It should be a wonderful trip. How long are you planning on being away?'

'Several weeks, at least. It's hardly worth going for less.' Grey eyes slanted her way. 'You and Paul ought to take off yourselves somewhere. It isn't as if he had any commitments to worry about. Why don't you suggest it? He'd probably jump at the idea.'

It was worth considering, Lisa told herself, conscious of reluctance. Away from St Amelia it was possible that she and Paul might recapture the emotions that had brought them together in the first place. Things were so different between them now. He still made love to her, but there was so little real communication. When it came right down to it, they had very few things in common. Paul was restless, always looking for some new interest. They had quarrelled bitterly before he had left this afternoon. He had called her dull and provincial and stormed off to look for what he had called 'some light relief'. Whether he would find it in Roadtown she had no idea.

'I might do that,' she said.

He was not yet back when they reached the house. Lisa took a leisurely shower and got into the white pants and shirt Madalyn herself had suggested as fitting wear for an evening sail, sliding her feet into narrow leather pumps in the absence of anything more suitable. Paul came in while she was fastening her hair up into a pony tail, viewing her with cynicism.

'Makes you look like some bit of a kid!'

Lisa didn't turn her head. 'In some sense, I suppose I'm not much more. Did you enjoy your trip?'

'Sure.' A faint smile crossed the handsome features. 'You should have come along.'

'You didn't appear to want me along,' she said. 'Dull and provincial, remember?'

'Is that what I called you?' He sounded more amused than apologetic. 'Poor little girl, left all alone by her big, bad husband!'

'I went riding with Madalyn,' she responded with deliberation. 'We called in on Kyle at the plant. Scott's coming over to dinner, then we're all going out in *Seajade*.'

'By all, I hope you're not including me.' He was stripping off his shirt as he spoke. 'I can't think of anything I'd rather do less.'

She said dully, 'In that case, I shan't go either.'

'Why on earth not? We don't have to live in each other's pockets, do we?' He kicked off his loafers on the way to the bathroom, leaving them where they fell. 'I'll keep Mother company. She can't stand sailboats either.'

Lisa remained where she was, gazing into the mirror at a pair of eyes filled with conflicting emotions. There was hurt, yes, but it lacked any depth. Go, Paul had said, so go she would. She hadn't realised until this moment how much she had been counting on making that trip this evening.

There was little comment over dinner when Paul announced his decision. It seemed to be taken for granted that Lisa would not be staying behind too. Weathering her mother-in-law's contemptuous glance, Lisa wondered what her reaction might be if she changed her mind and decided after all to stay with her husband. Whatever she did, it would be the wrong thing as far as the other was concerned.

The four of them drove over to the beach by jeep, the two girls in the back. In moonlight the sand looked pure silver, the gentle waves tipped with phosphorescence as they broke along the shoreline. The deck of the *Seajade* was solid teak, still warm from the sun. Lisa took a cockpit seat as they got under way, lifting her face to the night breeze in a sudden excess of well-being. For the first time in weeks she felt free. It was like coming out of a bad dream.

Madalyn had manoeuvred Scott up for'ard on some pretext or other, neither of them being any stranger to sailing. The manager seemed more relaxed tonight, Lisa thought: she had even heard him laugh at one or two of Madalyn's more outrageous sallies. He was a bit of a puzzle, she had to admit. Not at all the type one might expect to take on a job such as his.

'I wonder if he's running away from something,' she mused, and only realised she had spoken her thoughts aloud when Kyle glanced her way from his place at the helm.

'If you mean Scott, I'd say it's his business, wouldn't you?'

She flushed hotly. 'It was just idle curiosity. I wasn't intending asking him.'

'Good.' There was a pause, a sudden wry change of expression. 'That was uncalled for. Forget it.'

'No, you were quite right,' Lisa responded swiftly. 'It is his business.'

'A pity Madalyn can't see it the same way,' he said drily, eyes on the two up front. 'If I know my sister, she's pumping him right now. Not that she'll get much out of him. He never talks about the past.'

'It doesn't bother you that you don't know anything about him?' Lisa ventured.

'I know all I need to know. He does the job he's paid to do, that's all that matters to me.' There was another pause, another change of tone. 'Enjoying it so far?'

'It's wonderful!' She laughed. 'Of course, I can't say whether I'd be as good a sailor if the sea was rough.'

'We'll have to give you chance to find out.'

Her heart thudded suddenly, then steadied again. 'Paul isn't likely to change his mind, is he?'

'You're married to him,' came the level response. 'What do you think?' He glanced at her again when she made no answer. 'Not finding it such a sinecure?'

'I never expected it to be any sinecure,' she said huskily. 'Marriage needs working at, I know that.'

'Some more than others. You and Paul aren't in the least bit suited.' The statement was unequivocal. 'I imagine you're already beginning to realise that for yourself.'

She said with spirit, 'If I were really the little gold digger you first thought me it wouldn't matter so much, would it?'

Kyle laughed suddenly, teeth gleaming white against the night-darkened tan of his skin. 'You've got a point,' he admitted.

'Do you still believe it?' she asked after a moment, and felt his glance again.

'No. I think you were probably carried away by some romantic notion of love being all.'

'And Paul?'

'Paul?' The firm mouth had a cynical slant. 'He was making a gesture.'

Her voice came out low and unsteady. 'You're saying he

doesn't feel anything for me?'

'Of course he feels something. Few men could look at a lovely young thing like you and not feel anything. What I'd dispute is his readiness for marriage and all it entails—or should entail. He's too immature yet.'

Green eyes lifted. 'I suppose you could say the same about me.'

'Not in the same sense. I've watched you these past weeks. You're not happy, but you don't give way to it. Perhaps it's partly because you're cooped up here on St Amelia.'

'I don't feel cooped up,' Lisa denied. 'I love the island!'

Kyle studied her a moment, his expression difficult to define. 'I really think you mean that.'

'I do.' She was eager to convince him. 'Anyone would!'

'Hardly true. You're one in a thousand.'

She said softly, 'Will you be my friend now, Kyle, instead of my enemy?'

His smile held a hint of mockery, not, she thought, directed solely at her. 'I was never your enemy.'

'You've put up a very good imitation of it.'

'With reason.' He glanced at the compass and made some mental calculation. 'Did you bring a swimsuit?'

'Yes,' she acknowledged. 'Madalyn said we might have time for a swim.'

'Better go on down and change, then. We'll be coming up on the cays in a few minutes. You don't mind swimming in the sea at night?'

'I never tried it.' she laughed, feeling suddenly and exuberantly ready for anything. 'But I'm sure it will feel marvellous!'

Madalyn had already shown her round below decks. She undressed in one of the cabins, drawing on the one-piece white suit with a thrill of anticipation. This was the happiest she had felt in days, and all because Kyle had finally come round. With reason, he had said. She wondered what that meant. He was such a complex man; she doubted if she would ever quite understand him. And such a vitally attractive one too, came the thought unbidden to mind, sending a sudden small shiver the length of her spine.

They anchored for almost an hour off one of the tiny islets. Lisa was not a strong swimmer, but in water as calm and warm as this she felt no strain. Kyle made a point of staying close, giving her the confidence to strike out further than she would otherwise have done away from the boat. The water was a caress against her skin; she felt she could have stayed in it all night. Floating on her back, gazing at the star-sprinkled sky, she wanted for nothing at that moment.

'We should be getting back on board,' Kyle murmured lazily at her side.

'Just a few more minutes,' she begged. 'It's like being in a warm bath!'

'You can use one of the cars any time you want to get to the beach,' he said. 'It's no more than a ten-minute drive.'

'I never learned,' Lisa confessed, feeling inadequate again.

'Well, now's the time. Get Paul to show you the basics, then it's just a matter of gaining confidence. You're hardly going to come to much harm on St Amelia.'

'I've heard tell,' she responded on a light note, 'that driving lessons can spell death to a marriage.'

'All right, so I'll do the teaching.' He sounded tolerant. 'I'd hate to have that on my conscience.'

His sudden move to bring himself upright sent a small surge washing over Lisa's face. She choked and went under, swallowing more in the process. Panicking, she began to thresh, grasping frantically at Kyle when he reached for her.

'You're OK,' he said reassuringly against her ear,

treading water as he held her up. 'I won't let go of you until you're good and ready. Just take it easy.'

She felt safe there in his arms, yet her heart was pounding fit to burst. The pull of the water carried her body up against him, fitting it to the shape of him like two pieces of a jigsaw coming together. She saw his eyes flare in the moonlight, heard his sharply indrawn breath and bitten-off exclamation. When his mouth found hers she could only respond in kind, clinging to him, all thought suspended, not even caring when they both slid beneath the surface.

It was Kyle who broke it off, Kyle who brought them both back on even keel again in the water with strong thrusts of his leg muscles. Blindly, Lisa pressed herself away from him, beginning to swim towards the boat without thought of what she was doing. Despite the warmth of the water she was shivering all over. This wasn't real, a part of her mind kept telling her. In a few minutes she would wake up back at the house with Paul at her side in the double bed. It just wasn't real!

Kyle let her stay ahead of him, only surging forward at the last to pull himself up the ladder in advance of her and reach back to lend her a hand. She didn't want to touch him—didn't want him to touch her. The moment she was on deck she started for the hatch without looking at him.

'Don't run away,' he said softly.

The others were still in the water, and some distance away. Lisa paused in her headlong flight but didn't turn her head. 'It shouldn't have happened,' she forced out.

'It shouldn't, but it did.' He was close behind her; too close. She took another trembling step forward, freezing into immobility as his hand came down on her shoulder. 'Don't,' she pleaded. 'Let me go, Kyle!'

'I can't. Not this way.' Gently he turned her towards him, holding her there with both hands on her upper arms. His face looked austere in the silvery white light. 'It was just a kiss,' he said. 'Nothing else.'

He was lying, and they both knew it. The arousal had been mutual. Lisa could still feel her nipples standing proud beneath the flimsy covering of her suit, still retained the imprint of his body against her. In those few fleeting moments she had wanted him to make love to her the way Paul made love to her—only not the same either, because with Kyle it would be so very different; instinct told her that. He was mature the way Paul would never be mature; so much the man in command. Even now her body ached to be back in his arms, her mouth to feel the movement of his lips. She gazed at him with eyes gone wide and dark, her skin fluttering beneath his fingers. A muscle contracted sharply in his jaw.

'Don't look at me like that,' he said roughly, 'or I'm going to do it again.'

'No!' She drew back as far as he would let her, fighting her baser impulse. 'I'm married to your brother, Kyle!'

'Do you think I could forget?' His expression was rueful. 'You've been here a month, and there hasn't been a day when I've not wanted you. Why else do you think I've kept out of your way?'

'I thought it was because you despised me,' she said, low-toned. 'Just as your mother does.'

'I tried to persuade myself you were out for what you could get, only it was so obviously not true.' His grasp tautened a little. 'You're no more in love with Paul than he is with you, Lisa. I don't need to tell you that; you already know it for yourself. The pair of you acted on impulse—a bad impulse. If you'd gone to bed with him the way he wanted you might have realised he wasn't the right man for you in time.'

She said thickly, 'He told you that?'

His lips twisted. 'With Paul, few things are sacred. He'd have told me more if I'd been willing to listen. Blood might be thicker than water, but it doesn't run very warm between us, as you might have gathered. I was getting ready to pay him off when he turned up with you in tow. I'd do it still if I thought you and he could make anything of this marriage of yours.'

'Pay him off?'

'Buy him out, if that sounds better. I made the mistake of thinking I could change basic character. Mistakes have to be paid for.'

'I know.' She couldn't look at him. 'Let me go, Kyle. Please!'

'For now,' he said, complying. 'Only we're not going to leave it like this.' His tone roughened again. 'It's a hell of a situation, but we'll work something out. We have to if I want any peace of mind.'

He stayed on deck while she went below to change. Drying herself off, getting back into her clothes, she found that her thoughts kept going around in circles, getting nowhere. Paul and Kyle—the one her husband, the other a man she scarcely knew, yet felt more for. Not just physical, she told herself painfully. Kyle was the kind of man she should have married: someone she could lean on, rely on, respect as well as love. From the very first moment she had laid eyes on him she had known in her heart that her marriage was going to prove a failure. How could it be anything else when she was married to the wrong man?

Dwelling now on those moments she had spent locked in Kyle's arms, she felt her throat constrict. It mustn't happen again. He had too great an effect on her. With Paul there had always been a part of her that remained inviolate; with Kyle her senses told her there would be no restraint. He would possess his women completely.

She had to stop this, she told herself desperately. Her marriage might not be perfect but it was fact. Kyle was her brother-in-law, for God's sake! How could she have allowed herself to respond to him in that way? And Kyle himself was no better. She had to stay away from him, give him no further opportunity to undermine her principles. For better or worse, that had been one of the vows she had taken. She had to put some effort into attaining the first rather than the last.

She heard the others come back on board. When they all three came below she was making coffee in the galley.

'One thing I am proficient at,' she claimed when Madalyn offered to help. She avoided Kyle's eyes. 'It'll be ready by the time you're dressed.'

They drank it on deck before setting off back to St Amelia. 'We've got to do this again before I go,' said Madalyn lazily. 'I've really enjoyed tonight. Paul doesn't know what he's missed!'

'He's already tasted my coffee,' responded Lisa on a deliberately flippant note. 'We spent our honeymoon in a mountain chalet. I cooked him breakfast every morning.'

Madalyn gave her a swift sideways glance. 'Good for you. If Bella ever goes on strike we'll know who to call on. It takes me all my time to boil an egg!'

Kyle laughed. 'I remember the cake you once persuaded Bella to let you make!'

'Trust you.' She was laughing herself at the memory. 'I put in too much baking powder and the whole thing came up like a balloon until I opened the door. Sunk or not, I wasn't wasting all that effort. It went down all right with some fruit and cream in the middle.'

'Like lead,' agreed her brother. He drained his cup and rose lithely to his feet. 'Time we were making tracks.'

'You made the coffee, I'll do the washing up,' stated Madalyn firmly as Lisa reached for the empty mug. 'Scott can come and wipe.'

'All four of them?' he asked with irony, but he went anyway.

Kyle used the engine to take them clear of the cays before hoisting sail. The sheets cracked in the suddenly strengthened wind. 'We might be in for a bit of a blow tomorrow,' he observed. 'The glass is falling. Lucky it held off till now.' He paused as if awaiting some comment on Lisa's part, his glance brief but comprehensive. 'Feeling OK?'

'I'm not seasick,' Lisa responded, 'if that's what you mean.'

'Not entirely.' He glanced at her again, jaw firming. 'Lisa, it isn't ...'

'You were right the first time,' she cut in woodenly. 'It was just a kiss. Let's forget it.'

His shrug was dismissive. 'If that's what you want.'

What she wanted, Lisa thought miserably, had little bearing on what must be. Five weeks ago she had believed herself in love with Paul. How fickle could one get?

CHAPTER NINE

MADALYN's departure for Australia left a void Lisa knew was going to be difficult to fill, although she laughingly denied that fact when the former expressed concern.

'I'll be fine,' she affirmed. 'By the time you come back all the teething troubles will be over.' She indicated the waiting taxi. 'If you don't get going you'll miss your flight. You're quite sure you don't want us to come to the airport with you?'

'No, thanks. I hate prolonged goodbyes.' Madalyn got into the car, sticking her head out through the opened rear window. 'See you in about six weeks. Take care, now!'

She could take all the care in the world, reflected Lisa drily as she turned to make her way back to the launch, but she doubted if it was going to help. She and Paul were farther apart than ever, mostly, she was bound to admit, due to her own inability to pretend. Like making love to a block of wood, he had pronounced disgustedly only the previous night. It was fair enough comment, because that's what she had felt like.

The two of them had brought Madalyn across to Tortola in the launch—an offer made out of boredom more than anything else on Paul's part, Lisa privately considered. He had been talkative enough on the way over: she wondered if he would be the same once they were alone together. The way things were going, she might conceivably never see Madalyn again, because she didn't think she could stand another six weeks of it. Yet, if she left, where would she go? She didn't even have enough money of her own to buy herself an air ticket back to England, much less start a new life there. In any case, wasn't it a bit soon to be thinking of giving up? Marriage had to be worked at, she had told Kyle not so very long ago. She had hardly given it a chance.

Kyle. The very thought of him was enough to quicken her pulses. Living in the same house, seeing him every day, remembering the tumult he could rouse inside her—none of it helped. In fairness, he hadn't once attempted a repeat performance, nor had he indicated by word or glance that he even had any desires in that direction. There were times when she wondered if those moments when they had been alone together were figments of her imagination. Had he really kissed her in the sea that night, or was it all in her mind? Whichever, it made little difference in the long run because there could never be anything between them. The sooner she accepted that and stopped thinking of him in any way other than as Paul's brother, the better for all concerned. If only it were that easy.

Paul started up the launch engine as soon as he saw her coming. 'Thought you'd decided to go with her,' he commented as she came aboard.

Lisa slanted a glance at the handsome profile, conscious of the fact that it no longer did anything to her heart-strings. 'Would that have been a relief?'

He shrugged, swinging the boat out in a wide arc to clear a small sailing dinghy. 'We're not doing much for each other at present.'

'Perhaps we're not trying hard enough,' Lisa suggested, not really believing it as a solution herself.

'Or maybe we both need to take a break—give ourselves time to think things through.' He didn't wait for any reply. 'I might go over to St Thomas for a couple of days or so.'

'Leaving me on my own?'

'You wouldn't be on your own,' he said. 'There's Kyle—and Mother.'

Her laugh came short and brittle. 'Is that supposed to be some incentive?'

'If you don't like it,' on a suddenly impatient note, 'then make some other arrangement! The point is, I've already made mine.'

'When?' Her voice was low. 'I mean, when will you be leaving?'

'Tomorrow—or even this afternoon.' He shook his head as if repudiating an unspoken argument. 'It's for the best.'

'I'm sure you're right.' She added levelly, 'Would you like me to be gone when you get back?'

Blue eyes flicked her way, taking in her firm young curves under the brief sun-top, the slender length of sun-tanned leg revealed by sparkling white shorts. 'You've still got what it takes,' he said on a judicious note. 'I guess it's up to you to decide what you want to do with it. All I know is, you're not the same girl I married. Bring her back and I'll be happy enough.'

Would he? Lisa wondered. Two months ago, marriage itself had still held novelty value. That hardly applied any more. 'Madalyn thinks we should leave St Amelia and start up somewhere new,' she said without meaning to, and saw his expression harden again.

'She'd like to be rid of me too!'

'I'm sure that's not true.' Lisa was sorry now that she had spoken. 'She was thinking of you. After all, you can hardly pretend you enjoy living there.'

'My mother's there. Are you suggesting I should leave her?'

'No, of course not.' Lisa refrained from pointing out that he had been doing that anyway on a regular basis the past few years. She wasn't convinced it was any answer either. Where didn't matter, providing two people were happy to be together.

Whether Paul really had made previous plans or was

simply reacting to a sudden whim, he lost little time in organising his departure once they reached Tamarind. What he told his mother Lisa had no way of knowing, because he did it in private. The older Mrs Hamilton elected not to put in an appearance at lunch.

'Josh can take me straight through,' Paul said over coffee when she asked how he planned on travelling. 'It's only a few miles further. You can reach me at Frenchman's Reef if needs be.'

Don't go, Lisa suddenly wanted to beg. Don't desert me now. She bit her lip, aware that such a plea could only be justified if she could follow it up with sincere intent. She felt no differently about Paul: it was herself she was thinking of. To be alone with Kyle was the last thing she needed.

She didn't see him leave. Waving a fond goodbye seemed inappropriate under the circumstances. It should have been the other way round, she couldn't help thinking. She should have been the one leaving. Much as she loved it, Tamarind wasn't her home. She didn't have a home.

Kyle arrived home earlier than usual to find her stretched out listlessly in the sun. He heard her unemotional explanation of Paul's whereabouts without comment other than an ironic tilt of a lip, diving into the pool to swim several lengths in his effortless crawl before coming back to join her.

'That got rid of a few cobwebs,' he said, towelling his hair. 'It's time somebody round here took matters in hand. How badly has that brother of mine hurt you?'

'It isn't his fault,' Lisa said dully, without opening her eyes. 'No more than mine, anyway. It's been said often enough, hasn't it?'

'What has?'

'"Marry in haste, repent at leisure". Clichés only become clichés because they're so true.'

'Maybe.' There was a pause before he said softly, 'What

first attracted you to Paul, Lisa?'

This time her eyes did come open, though only to stare at the sky. 'His looks, I suppose.'

'Nothing else?'

She gave a faint sigh. 'It was a different world from what I'd been used to—so glamorous and exciting! I could hardly believe it when he picked me out of all the girls he could have chosen to spend his time with.'

'You obviously had something they didn't,' came the dry response. 'Like the ability to say no, perhaps.'

Lisa said thickly, 'You really think that was the only reason he asked me to marry him?'

'I think it was one reason. Paul never could stand being denied anything. If he couldn't get it one way he'd find another.'

Her laugh sounded cracked. 'I must have been a terrible disappointment to him. He thinks I'm frigid.' She coloured immediately. 'I'm sorry, I shouldn't have said that.'

Kyle's tone was level, without censure. 'You're far from frigid. I can vouch for that.'

'Don't.' She was too mortified to try concealing her reaction. 'I'd rather not remember that night.'

'I find it impossible to forget.' His voice had softened. 'I remember standing in the doorway that first time I saw you, wondering who you were and if the fact that you were obviously far too young for me was going to make any difference. I'd just about decided I wasn't going to let it when you told me you were already married to my brother. If I came down heavy on you it was mostly because he'd found you first.'

Lisa was very still, hardly daring to breathe. 'Do you still think I'm too young?' she heard herself ask.

'In years, perhaps.' Kyle reached out and ran his fingers lightly down her arm, smiling at her involuntary shudder.

'Not in any other way. When are you due to be twenty-one?'

The question took her by surprise, realisation even more so. 'The fourteenth,' she said. 'That's next week, isn't it?'

'Yes, it is.' He sounded odd. 'Why didn't you tell us before this? Madalyn would have postponed her trip if she'd known.'

'I'd forgotten myself,' she confessed, sitting up on the lounger.

'Your twenty-first!' on a sceptical note.

'It's true. I just hadn't thought about it.' She avoided his eyes. 'I've had a lot of other things on my mind lately.'

'Well, it's not too late.' The pause was brief. 'When did Paul say he'd be back?'

'He didn't, but he should be—back, I mean.' Lisa made a wry little gesture. 'It doesn't really matter, does it? Not the way things are.'

'We're not going to just let it pass because things aren't working out the way they might have. That will sort itself out in time.'

She looked at him then, eyes darkened by an emotion she no longer tried to conceal. 'How can it?'

His hands came out to cup her face, drawing her towards him until he could reach her lips. The kiss left her trembling, yearning for more. 'We'll find a way,' he promised.

She was treading the path to more heartache, Lisa knew, yet she couldn't bring herself to turn her back on the feelings Kyle roused in her. Love involved so much more than just wanting to be with someone. It meant placing trust, opening up the heart. Paul had been an infatuation, she could see that now. The mistake she had made was in not giving it time to wear off. Kyle was something else entirely—a man she could give herself to unreservedly. Yet he was forbidden to her, wasn't he?

'Stop thinking about it,' Kyle advised, watching her face. 'As soon as Paul gets back the two of you can get down to doing some serious talking. You made a mistake but it isn't irreversible.'

'We can hardly start thinking about divorce after two months,' Lisa protested weakly.

'I agree under present British law it isn't going to be a feasible proposition for some time. That's something else that would have to be worked out.' He straightened abruptly. 'Come on in for a swim. It will take your mind off things.'

Nothing could, she thought, but she went anyway. Just being with Kyle was a solace of sorts.

Paul did not return in a couple of days, nor even in three. Only when she received the cable from Caracas did it become clear to Lisa that he had never had any intention of making it a short trip.

Absence makes the heart grow fonder, he had written. *See you in a couple of weeks.*

That Elaine Hamilton had not been *au fait* with her son's plans was made obvious by her reception of the news. She accused Lisa of driving him away, working herself up into a blind tirade until Kyle stepped in and calmed her down with a few tersely spoken words.

'She's taking this whole thing too far,' he said after she had left them. 'I'm not sure which is worse—possessive mothers or irresponsible offspring!'

'Perhaps one creates the other,' Lisa suggested, still shaking from the viciousness of the attack. 'I didn't realise she felt quite so much hatred towards me.'

'It isn't just you as a person,' he said. 'She'd have been the same with any girl he sprang on her that way.'

'But she must have realised he'd probably get married one day.'

'To a girl she'd chosen for him, perhaps. One she could control.' He touched her cheek with the back of a knuckle, his first caress since the day Paul had left. 'Don't hate her too much.'

'I don't,' she said softly. She hesitated before adding, 'Don't you ever feel resentful of the way she is over Paul?'

He shrugged. 'I suppose I'm as much to blame for that as anybody. Dad and I were very close. The only reason she told me the truth about Paul was to underline how much Dad had loved her. She couldn't grasp that it took nothing away from me.' Grey eyes studied her reflectively. 'It shouldn't be too difficult to find out just where Paul is. He could still be back here in time for your birthday.'

Lisa bit her lip. 'I'd rather he didn't know. I'd rather no one knew!'

'*I* know,' he reminded her. 'We could always make it a private celebration.' His smile made her tingle. 'How about spending the day on *Seajade*?'

She gave herself no time to consider the offer. 'I'd like that.'

'Then it's settled. We'll leave before breakfast and eat on the boat. How are you with bacon and eggs?'

'Ready, willing and able,' she laughed. 'You already approved my coffee.'

'So I did.' Just for a moment something sparked in his eyes. 'I'll look forward to repeating the experience.'

Wakening to a birthday morning without cards was no new experience for Lisa. Her aunt had not been one for making much of a fuss over anniversaries, although she had managed to remember her eighteenth. It all seemed so long ago, Lisa reflected now, looking out of the window at the sun-kissed landscape. She hated the thought of leaving all this warmth and beauty, of looking for a job and a place to live, of being alone again with no one in the world to turn to—all of which must happen if she separated from Paul.

Yet she could hardly do anything else under the circumstances, could she? This marriage of theirs had never stood a chance of succeeding from the first. Kyle or no Kyle, it would have turned out the same in the end.

Leaving him was going to be the hardest part of all, she acknowledged painfully. Even if he meant what he had said about seeing her first, it made little difference. She could scarcely divorce one man and marry his brother instead. If she were sensible she'd be packing her bags right this minute instead of contemplating spending the whole day in his company. Only she wasn't sensible. This might very well be her only opportunity to be with him. It was beyond her to pass it up.

He was waiting for her in one of the jeeps out front when she went down. It had rained in the night and the air smelled fresh and clean, the scents only just beginning to permeate.

'Happy birthday,' he said softly as she climbed in beside him. He leaned across to kiss her, his lips light yet warm. 'You look radiant!'

She felt it. Kyle would illuminate any female heart, she thought. She was going to enjoy today and forget about tomorrow. Let time stand still for once.

Time didn't, of course. They took the *Seajade* out into the wide open ocean, heading towards St Croix forty miles away. The weather was calm, the sea gentle in its motion. Lying on top of the cabin, soaking up the sun, Lisa thought she had never been more content.

Like breakfast, lunch consisted of food brought from the house. He only used the refrigerator, Kyle said, when he was planning an extended trip. Lisa imagined what it must be like to spend days, even weeks, sailing wherever the fancy led, putting into different ports, seeing new places. But most of all she imagined the togetherness of two people sharing those days and nights, making love under the stars with the boat gently rocking beneath them, braving the elements when they took a turn for the worse. The woman Kyle eventually married would have all that—and more. Why couldn't it have been her?

'You've gone very quiet,' Kyle commented, finishing off the last of the coffee. 'I thought today we were going to forget all that.'

'It wasn't Paul I was thinking about,' she confessed. 'Just how wonderful all this is and how grateful I am to you for bringing me—and for the lovely present!'

'I don't want your gratitude.' His voice had acquired a faint roughness. 'I want *you*, Lisa.'

Her heart was thudding loud enough to almost drown out the music coming from the radio. 'I'm not . . . free,' she got out.

'I don't care.' The grey eyes held a determined light. 'Paul doesn't deserve you.'

He's still my husband, she wanted to say, but the words wouldn't come. When Kyle reached for her she went too readily into his arms, shutting out all thought of Paul, of her marriage, of everything except for the emotions of right here and now.

His mouth was a source of endless pleasure, his lips teasing hers apart, drawing her up into a spiral of sheer sensation, his tongue gently questing until she answered in kind, her body pressing closer, her breath shortening, deepening, breaking up into shuddering little gasps as the wildness grew inside her. She was wearing the briefest of bikinis, held only by strings at hip and centre back. When he took it off she felt no sense of embarrassment, only pride that her body could bring that look to his eyes as he scanned it. She trembled when he touched her, but she wanted that touch, the same way she wanted his lips at her throat, at her breast, kissing their way over every inch of her until she could scarcely bear another moment of waiting for what was to come.

At some point, she never knew which, he removed his trunks. The feel of his naked body against her was wonderful. Tanned though she was, his thighs made hers look almost white by contrast, the hardness of them pressuring hers to open, to take him, to tremble in response as they slid together and became one being. This was the way it should be, she thought hazily. So totally and completely right. Then he began to move and the whole world began to spin, taking her with it into a vortex of sensation so exquisite it jerked a cry from her lips, tearing her apart with its force, with its power, until a million arc lights went off in her head and everything ceased to exist.

It was like coming back from the dead, she thought dazedly when her senses began to function again. Never in her wildest dreams could she have imagined the actuality of true fulfilment. Not Paul's fault, she knew that now. He simply wasn't the right man for her. With Kyle it was so different. He made her let go. She wanted him again, now, this very moment. Her whole body was trembling with the need.

Kyle lifted his head to look at her, eyes softened, satiated. 'You're delicious, do you know that?'

'I'm glad.' She eased her body beneath him, smiling to see the sudden flare of expression. 'You're heavy.'

'Do you want me to move?' he asked.

'No,' she admitted. Emotion swamped her as she gazed up into the lean features. 'Oh, God,' she said despairingly, 'this can't be right!'

He bent his head swiftly and found her lips, kissing her into a state where she didn't know right from wrong—and no longer cared. 'I'm not interested in the moral issues,' he said hardily. 'You and Paul were never going to make it as a couple. As soon as he gets back we're going to start sorting this whole mess out. Don't ask me how. I haven't got round to that aspect yet.'

Lisa reached up and kissed him hungrily, feeling his response. She wanted to tell him she loved him, only it was too soon, too close to the day she had used those same words to his brother. It was different now because she knew what love really was, but it was still too soon. He hadn't actually said he loved her, if it came to that, only that he wanted her. She had to trust that the two were synonymous in his mind where she was concerned. Yet love couldn't conquer all, regardless of what was said. She was married to his brother and would be for some time to come, even if both of them agreed to conclude the pretence. In the meantime, she could hardly stay on at Tamarind.

It was just as good the second time. Lying secure in Kyle's arms afterwards, Lisa could only try to convince herself that it would all come right in the end. This man was all she wanted in the whole world. Was it too much to ask?

'We're going to have to stir ourselves,' he said with reluctance after several more moments of lying there. 'The horizons were clear when I set the steering vane, but they might not be now.' He laughed at the sudden alarm in her eyes. 'I doubt if anybody would get close enough to spy on us. Even if they did, we're not doing anything out of the ordinary.'

Lisa sat up slowly as he got to his feet, thankful to find the immediate vicinity of the boat still empty of life. Some large vessel stood far out on the horizon, white hull catching the sun. She wished suddenly and desperately that they could just sail away into that same distance.

'If only today need never end!' she exclaimed, then blushed at the sheer romanticism of the thought. 'Impractical, I know.'

'Dreams usually are. It doesn't make them any less enticing.' Kyle made no attempt to re-don his trunks, quite unabashed by his nudity as he adjusted the rigging. Lisa admired the strong, clean lines of his body, the ripple of muscle under the smooth skin of his back, the hardness of thigh. He made Paul seem so young, so undeveloped, not just in physique but in every way. Just looking at Kyle now, Lisa was shaken by the depth of her emotions. She wanted to belong to him completely, utterly: his to cherish for ever more.

'Life's so unfair,' she said on a bitter note.

'Life's what we make it,' he returned. 'Paul opted out on his responsibilities, so I'm taking matters into my own hands. We're going to forget about him for this next couple of weeks. When he gets back will be time enough to start putting things in order. Until then it's just the two of us.' He held out a hand to her, smile inviting. 'Come on down here.'

'Like this?' she asked a little shyly, and he laughed.

'I can't think of any other way I'd rather see you!' He watched her as she rose with some reticence still to her feet, her hand clasping the mast for support. The flame was there again in his eyes. 'You're beautiful,' he said, so softly that the words were drowned by the slapping of the waves, but she read the shape of them on his lips and felt the last barrier drop. She reached him without a single stumble on the way.

For Lisa there was agony as well as ecstasy in those two short weeks. By tacit consent they had no physical contact within the house itself, but took *Seajade* out almost every day. She lived for those hours, suffering the rest. It was only when she was alone with Kyle that she could shut out the knowledge of what eventually had to come. Leave it to him, Kyle had said, yet how could she? She had to tell Paul herself—make him understand. He didn't love her any more than she loved him, but that wasn't to say he was going to find it easy to accept the situation as it stood. How might she herself have felt had it been Paul who had fallen for her sister, say?

If Mrs Hamilton had any suspicion of what was going on between her son and her daughter-in-law she kept her own counsel. Lisa avoided her as much as possible. The other woman could only be delighted if the marriage of which she so disapproved broke up, but she could hardly be expected to react with quite the same emotions to the discovery that her elder son was involved in the affair. Lisa herself deplored her own behaviour, but she couldn't stop it. Kyle was in her blood, as necessary to her as breathing. How she was going to cope when deprived of him she dared not even allow herself to consider.

Kyle's announcement towards the end of the second week that he himself had to go away for a day or two came like a thunderbolt.

'It's business,' he said. 'Needs must. I'll be back before Paul gets home, never fear.'

'What's going to happen then?' Lisa asked dully. 'I can hardly stay on here, can I?'

'I suppose not.' His head was averted, eyes studying the cloud build up astern. 'There's a squall coming up fast. You'd better get below if you don't want to get wet.'

Lisa shook her head. 'I'd rather be up here.'

'OK, but the temperature's likely to drop a few points. You'll find a reefer hanging behind my cabin door.'

'What about you?' she asked.

'I've been wet before. It isn't likely to last long.'

The jacket was where he had said. Lisa took it down and slid her arms into the sleeves, warming to the thought that Kyle had been the last one to wear it before her. One of the small buttons edging the sleeves was hanging by a thread. She pulled it free, slipping it into the pocket of her jeans to keep it safe. Later, after the squall had passed, she would stitch it back on. It gave her pleasure to do things like that for Kyle, minor though they were. There were so few opportunities.

She could see the rain sweeping in over the water as she emerged through the hatch, feel the chill in the wind. It hit them seconds later, a regular deluge boiling the sea around them and plastering Kyle's thin shirt to his body. Visibility was nil. Lisa ducked back under cover for the duration, hugging the jacket about her. The force of the rain took her breath away. It seemed it must swamp the boat. To be at sea in a real storm must be a terrifying experience, she thought, although with Kyle at the helm it might also prove an exhilarating one. He responded to challenge.

Miraculously the skies cleared again within minutes. Steam began rising from the deck boards in the renewed heat of the sun. Lisa took a towel out to Kyle to dry his dripping hair, watching him as he rubbed the dark thickness. Tomorrow and the next day she would be without him. She didn't know how she was going to bear the parting.

'You never answered the question,' she said huskily. 'What's going to happen when Paul gets back?'

'That depends largely on Paul himself.' His tone was level. 'I can't predict how he'll react.'

'But whatever happens, I'm going to have to leave the island.'

'Only as far as Tortola. We'll get you an apartment.'

'Where you can come and visit me?'

He slid a hand round the back of her neck, his fingers warm against her skin. 'Lisa, we have to face facts. The only alternative is for you to go back to England and wait for matters to take their course. Would you prefer that?'

'No,' she admitted, and sighed. 'I just can't see there ever being a time when we can be together openly, that's all. Not on St Amelia, at any rate.'

He studied her face, an odd expression in his eyes. 'Are

you suggesting I make a choice?'

'No, of course not,' she denied. 'It's your home. All I meant was that with Paul there it would be difficult—wouldn't it?'

He made no attempt to argue the point. 'I could follow my original inclinations and buy his share back from him,' he said. 'He'd probably jump at the chance to move out for good.'

'And your mother?'

'If Paul went it's doubtful if she'd want to stay.' There was a tinge of irony in his voice. 'You think Madalyn might be any problem?'

Lisa flushed. 'That's unfair!'

'Yes, it is.' He brought her up closer and kissed her, expression rueful. 'It's going to take time and patience, but we'll get there in the end. Just bear with me.'

'I can bear anything,' she said shakily, 'except losing you.'

'You won't do that,' he promised, and then on a softer note, 'Let's go below.'

He left the next morning. Faced with the long, lonely hours, Lisa drove over to the plant and talked Scott into finding her something to do. He asked no questions, but she wondered how much he guessed. Like Kyle, he was a man not easily read.

With all three of her offspring away, there had seemed every likelihood that Mrs Hamilton senior would elect to steer clear of any unessential contact. Lisa was unprepared to find her at the dinner table that evening. Her attempts at light conversation were met with a stony contempt that soon reduced her to silence. She picked listlessly at her food, miserably aware that matters could only get worse when the truth came to light.

'You don't really think you're going to get anywhere with Kyle, do you?' the older woman said suddenly and vindictively over coffee. 'He said from the start he'd break this marriage up. I'm not saying I approve of his methods, but he's shown you for what you are. Did you really imagine you could fool him the way you fooled Paul?'

'I didn't try to fool Paul,' Lisa denied as calmly as she was able. 'We both made the mistake.'

Elaine leapt on the words. 'Then you admit it was a mistake?'

There was no point, Lisa reflected, in denying it. 'Yes,' she said.

'After deciding that Kyle was the better proposition.'

'It wasn't like that.' Lisa made a helpless little gesture. 'It really wasn't!'

The scorn remained. 'You made another mistake when you set your sights on Kyle. He's going to send you packing as soon as he gets back.'

Lisa stared at her, eyes darkened. 'I don't believe you.'

'No? Well, wait and see. Oh, you won't be left penniless, I'm sure. Providing you leave St Amelia, he'll no doubt see you well enough provided for. He's probably arranging the financial aspect right now. He told me he'd be seeing his lawyers.'

Lisa pressed herself unsteadily to her feet. She felt torn, wanting to disbelieve yet unable to be totally sure of her ground. 'You're just guessing,' she accused. 'You can't know for certain what his intentions are!'

'I know my son. Like his father, he's capable of being quite ruthless. He wanted you gone: he wouldn't care how he managed it.' Her voice took on an added malice. 'Especially if he could get something out of it on the side. After all, you're a very attractive young woman.'

Blindly, Lisa turned and walked away from the table. It wasn't true, she kept telling herself, but there was no real conviction in it. It would explain so much—the suddenness with which Kyle had changed towards her, for instance. He hadn't deemed her worthy of subtlety, and he had been right. He had been using her, that was all: how he must have laughed at her sheer gullibility!

She had to get away from this place, she thought. At the very least she could save herself that much humiliation. Too late tonight, of course. Tomorrow would have to do. She would pack just the bare essentials: the rest could be sent on when she knew where she was going to be. As for Kyle's financial arrangements, she wanted none of it. She'd get a job of some kind.

There was little difficulty in deciding what to take because she simply grabbed the first items to hand in drawers and wardrobe. The sight of her white drill jeans brought back memories she would have preferred to forget. Blinking back the moisture gathering at the back of her eyes, she reached into the pocket and drew out the blue button she had never found time to stitch back on, cupping it for a moment in the palm of her hand. A part of her urged her to drop it, to kick it out of sight under the bed, but she couldn't bring herself to make the move. In the end she tucked it away inside her writing-case. In time to come it would serve to remind her not to indulge in foolish dreams, she thought cynically. If she needed a reminder after this.

She lay tossing and turning through the early hours, finally falling into an exhausted slumber around five. Waking to the sight of her packed suitcase standing ready and waiting by the dressing-table brought instant depression to join the headache thudding behind her eyes. No nightmare, but reality. She was never going to see Kyle again.

It was already ten o'clock, she noted with dismay as she pressed herself reluctantly upright. There was little chance that Kyle would be back today, but she couldn't risk it. No way could she bear to face him again. She would have to ask for the use of the launch to take her across to Tortola, but she envisaged little protest on that score from her mother-in-law. From Tortola she would take the shuttle to St Thomas and a plane for home.

Her heart lurched sickeningly as she suddenly remembered her lack of available funds. A swift glance at her cheque stubs confirmed that she had approximately one hundred and sixty pounds to her name. That wasn't going to get her far. The obvious solution was to ask Mrs Hamilton for help, only that was beyond her. St Thomas was US territory: it was unlikely that she was going to be able to stay there very long. All the same, it would have to do for the present. She would work something out, even if it meant stowing away on board a ship or something. The main thing was just to be off this island when Kyle returned.

She chose a dress at random from the wardrobe, fastening the belt about her slender waist without so much as a glance in the mirror. Paul came into the room as she slid her feet into a pair of shoes, and paused in the doorway to view her with lifted brows.

'Going somewhere?'

Lisa looked back at him dispassionately, too numb to even feel surprise at his unexpected return. 'How long have you been back?'

'A few minutes,' he acknowledged, closing the door behind him. 'I caught the first shuttle and phoned through for the launch from Roadtown.'

'Then you haven't seen your mother yet?'

'No.' His forehead creased. 'Should I have?'

She said slowly, 'I think she may have something she wants to tell you.'

'About what?'

'Me.' She paused, swallowing on the dryness in her throat. 'And Kyle.'

The skin around his mouth whitened as his teeth came

together. 'And is it true?'

'Yes.' She shook her head as he made to speak. 'Don't pretend it hurts anything except your pride, Paul. We were finished before you went away.'

'And that gives him the right to take over?'

'*I* gave him the right,' she said, chin lifting. 'I'm not making any excuses. It happened, that's all.'

For a moment the blue eyes retained their fierce light, then slowly changed character. His shoulders lifted in a hard shrug. 'So you made it with my brother. I'll remember to commiserate with him when I see him.'

Lisa ignored the shaft. Paul had no power to hurt her. 'I want to leave,' she declared steadily. 'It seems the best thing all round.'

It was a moment before he replied: she could see the calculation in his gaze. 'Are you saying you want a divorce?' He asked at length.

'It looks that way.' She gave a faint smile. 'It's time we faced up to it, Paul. We don't belong together.'

He said softly, 'You think you'd be better off with Kyle?'

Lisa steeled herself against pain. 'I think we'd all be better off apart.'

'I'm sure you're right.' He glanced in the direction of the suitcase. 'Where will you go?'

'As far as I can,' she said. 'I don't have much money.'

'That's no problem.' He shook his head at her sound of protest. 'It's the least I can do. After all, I was the one who did the proposing in the first place.' His mouth tilted. 'Not one of my better impulses.'

'Nor mine,' she agreed. Her hesitation was brief: she really had no choice. 'All right, you can buy me a ticket home to England.'

'For starters?' he suggested cynically.

She said with emphasis, 'I shan't be wanting anything else from you, Paul. I can make my own way. It's going to be some time before we're actually free agents again, but we don't need to have any personal contact while we're waiting.'

He was looking at her as if he had never really seen her properly before. 'You've altered,' he said. 'You even sound different.'

'It's called decisiveness.' She glanced at her watch. 'I can make the afternoon flight to New York if I get moving now. I'll have to borrow the launch.'

'I'll take you,' Paul offered. 'I'll need to sort out the ticket business, anyway.' He sounded suddenly buoyant, as if a load had been lifted from his mind. 'Mother doesn't need to know I've been home yet. I'll surprise her at dinner.'

And delight her too, reflected Lisa with a cynicism of her own. She no longer cared. All she wanted was to be away from St Amelia and its memories.

They were on St Thomas by two-thirty. Lisa had been surprised when Paul insisted on taking her all the way through but he had remained adamant. Probably wanted to make sure she actually left the islands, she told herself. And why not?

The hire of a car to take them to the airport seemed a ridiculous waste of both time and money when taxis were so readily available. Paul waved to a couple crossing the road as they drove through the town, not bothering to explain who they were. He was whistling under his breath, revealing a lack of concern for the coming parting which might have been insulting had Lisa been capable of feeling anything at the time. The pain would come later during the long hours in the air when there was nothing else to do but think.

At no point had she considered the possibility that the flight might already be fully booked. As it turned out, there was only the one spare seat in tourist class. Saying goodbye

to Paul was more awkward than hurtful, especially when
he thrust the thick bundle of notes into her hand.

'Take it,' he urged. 'You're going to need something. Let
me know where you are as soon as you're fixed up with a
place to stay, and we'll get things under way.' There was a
certain ruefulness in the blue eyes as he looked at her. 'Sorry
it had to end like this. Take care of yourself, Lisa.'

'And you,' she said.

She landed at Heathrow at eight-thirty the following
morning, taking the train through to Victoria where she
planned on leaving her suitcase while she looked for
somewhere to stay. She had slept little on the plane, which,
combined with the previous night's restlessness, had left her
drained. A change of clothing might improve matters, she
thought on the way. She could use the ladies' cloakroom,
and have a wash and brush-up while she was about it.

There was no attendant on duty when she got there, and
the roller towels had not been changed for days, judging
from their state. Lisa opened up her case on the floor for
want of anywhere else to rest it, sorting through the
contents for something simple and crease-free. At least the
sun was shining outside. That was a bonus in itself. A skirt
and blouse would probably be the easiest—plus a pair of
flatter sandals for walking.

The two middle-aged women who had come into the
cloakroom shortly after her were taking their time. Lisa
could hear them whispering to each other as she stood up
straight again. Not exactly a prepossessing pair, she
thought without especial interest, running water into one of
the bowls. They both looked as if a good wash wouldn't go
amiss. Not that the facilities here were any aid. She was
going to have to use the box of tissues from her case in order
to dry herself with any degree of hygiene. From the sublime
to the ridiculous, came the dull thought. This was her life
from now on. She had to forget the rest.

It was when she bent to splash water over her face that the two women went into action. She felt a hand come down heavily on the back of her neck, pushing her whole face down into the water so that she couldn't breathe. Frantically, she kicked backwards, feeling her heel connect with a shin-bone and hearing the string of curses as the grip on her neck momentarily eased. As her eyes came level with the mirror above, she caught a brief glimpse of a vicious face beneath the unkempt mop of dirty hair, then something hit her on the side of the head and the world exploded into a trillion bright stars . . .

CHAPTER TEN

IT took the sudden, stinging downpour of rain to jerk Lisa out of the past. She had brought the jeep to a stop on a spit of land overlooking the sea, with the nearest belt of trees several hundred feet away. By the time she reached them both she and the car were wet. Not that it mattered too much. Rain rarely lasted any length of time, and the sun would soon dry her off.

It felt strange being in full possession again—like having a split personality, in some ways. With little difference in conclusions though, she thought painfully. Kyle had never said the words because he had never felt the emotion. Not where she was concerned. The first time he had been intent on breaking up his brother's inopportune marriage, the second on securing his land. He could have had the latter without marrying her, had he only realised it. She would have made him a present of it for the asking.

So what were they left with? Physically, the marriage had everything going for it. For Kyle that might even be enough. Only not for her. Without love to back it, passion soon faded. She had proved that already with Paul. Could she bear to see that light go out of his eyes, to sense his gradual loss of interest until making love to her became little more than a token gesture? He had shown no compassion for Imogen's feelings: why should he care about hers?

Thunder rolled overhead. Way out to sea a line of blue appeared above the horizon, pushing the cloud before it as it reached out for the land. The rain ceased as abruptly as it had begun and the sun broke through, glistening the dripping branches.

One thing she couldn't do was sit here for the rest of the day, Lisa acknowledged. Not unless she wanted a search party out looking for her. What she had to decide, and quickly, was her course of action from this point on. As far as Kyle was concerned, the past was still a closed book to her. Telling him the truth would gain her nothing. The alternative was no solution either, if she looked at it rationally. She had already run out on one marriage: this time she had to stay and face up to the situation.

The jeep Kyle always used was standing in the yard when she reached the house. He came out as she parked, waiting with hands thrust into the pockets of his shorts until she reached him.

'I was coming to look for you,' he said. 'That's the first time you've taken a car.'

'The others were out riding and it seemed a good time to try it.' Lisa couldn't make herself meet the grey eyes directly. 'I sheltered from the rain.' She added brightly, 'Where is everyone?'

His regard had sharpened a little. 'Madalyn said you went up to see Mother. Did she upset you in any way?'

Lisa avoided the question. 'She simply wanted to tell me we'd be free to move into her rooms after tomorrow.'

'The point scarcely needed making.' It was obvious he wasn't fully convinced. 'How do you feel about it?'

'I don't really see the need,' she said carelessly. 'Did you bring Scott back with you?'

'I asked him. He said he had things to do.'

'He probably can't bear seeing Madalyn with Tod.'

'Maybe.' The tone was non-committal. 'They're down at the pool. Are you ready to eat?'

'Give me five minutes,' she said. 'These things are still damp. I'll see you down there.'

She ran on into the house before he could comment. When she reached the room they shared she was breathing as fast as if she had just taken part in a marathon, her heart thudding painfully against her rib-cage. It was going to be difficult, if not impossible, to act as if everything was the same. Kyle already suspected something was wrong. His mother was unlikely to tell him the truth if he asked her. She had sown her seeds: they needed no further nurturing.

Changing her shorts and sun-top for clean ones in a bright singing yellow, she tried to be sensible about things. All right, so Kyle had not been entirely honest with regard to his motives, but what harm had he actually done her? Her feelings for him weren't worth a great deal if they couldn't withstand a little disillusionment. The only way to handle things was to carry on as before, and hope for eventual reciprocation. Kyle wanted her physically: that had to be a good starting-point. It was up to her to make him feel more deeply than that.

The sight of her mother-in-law already seated at the luncheon table strengthened her will to dissemble. Not for anything would she give her the satisfaction of knowing how deeply her words had cut. She was sufficiently in command of herself to withstand Kyle's searching glance with a smile on her lips. Her marriage to Paul had lasted two months: this one was for life—unless Kyle himself ever told her to go. Not exactly the heaven she had envisaged this past few days, but a great many women would give their all to be where she was, even so.

'They're putting on a barbecue in town tonight,' Kyle said casually towards the end of the meal. 'Anybody fancy going?'

'Sounds good,' said Tod. 'Why don't we all go?' He didn't look in Madalyn's direction as he added, 'Might get that manager of yours to loosen up a mite. Couldn't get anything out of him this morning when we met up.'

'He's not much for socialising,' Kyle acknowledged. 'I can ask him.'

'I shan't be going, of course,' put in his mother. 'I'll be leaving early. Joshua can take me to Roadtown,' she added without inflection.

'I'm taking you through to St Thomas,' stated her son. 'That means you don't need as early a start.'

'There's no necessity . . .' she began.

'I think there is. It's been a long time since you last left the island.'

'I'd like to come with you,' Lisa offered on impulse, and received a sharpened blue glance.

'Making sure I don't change my mind at the last minute?'

Lisa put a restraining hand on Kyle's arm as he made a sharp movement. 'This is your home far more than it's mine,' she said levelly. 'I'd be more than happy if you decided to stay.'

Elaine was the first to drop her gaze. She looked disconcerted. 'Do as you like,' she muttered. 'It doesn't matter to me.' She pushed back her chair with an abrupt movement. 'I still have some packing to finish off.'

Tod broke the pause after her departure by saying heartily, 'What say we go sailing this afternoon? Unless you'd other plans made, Kyle?' he added as an afterthought.

The latter shook his head. 'With Scott around, I'm pretty much free to please myself.'

'I'll give it a miss, if you don't mind.' Lisa had said it before she even finished forming the thought, weathering the surprised glances with a faint smile and an apologetic shake of her head. 'I don't feel too good, and I want to be fit for tonight.'

'You only picked at your lunch,' Kyle observed, studying

her thoughtfully. 'Not coming down with anything, I hope?'

'I don't think so.' She felt a fraud, but the memories of all that had happened between them on board the *Seajade* were too intrusive at present. 'Just a bit of an off-day, I expect. No reason why the rest of you shouldn't go. I'll lie down for an hour.'

'Couldn't think of it!' exclaimed Tod.

'We're not going to do her any good hanging around,' said Madalyn on a note of practicality. 'When I feel off the hooks all I want is to be left alone. I'm sure Lisa feels the same way? Right?' with a smile in her sister-in-law's direction. 'Unless you'd rather Kyle kept you company?'

'No.' The denial was too hasty: she tried to amend it. 'I mean, you're right. I just need to be on my own. It will soon pass.' The strain was beginning to tell on her. She stood up, smile over-bright. 'See you all later.'

Kyle made no attempt to follow her, but she could feel his eyes on her as she walked away. He wasn't deceived. Not wholly. But he was letting it go for now. The thought of being with him again—of making love—brought a sensation akin to panic. She was going to need to be very much on top of her emotions by then.

Night had fallen before the sailing party returned. Lisa took care to be dressed and seated out on the veranda with a book to hand. Yes, she responded in answer to Tod's solicitous enquiry, she was feeling quite restored and ready to enjoy the barbecue.

'Did you manage to get in touch with Scott about coming?' she asked Kyle.

'I rang through before we left,' he confirmed. 'He said he might.'

'Which means no.' Madalyn's tone was flat. 'We'd all better get our skates on if we want to eat. Don't wear your Bermudas, Tod. They really do nothing for a man.'

'Now she tells me.' He sounded wryly humorous. 'I'll wear jeans, OK?'

'Sure.' She was already moving on indoors, her disinterest plain to all.

'There are times,' Kyle observed to no one in particular, 'when a good swift kick in the pants might be beneficial!'

Tod laughed. 'Only a brother might risk it!'

Madalyn was being deliberately hurtful, Lisa reflected when she was alone again. It wasn't like her. Far from telling Tod the truth, she seemed to be trying to alienate him. She felt sorry for the man, yet she could to a great extent understand and sympathise with what Madalyn was going through. They were both victims of their own feminine weaknesses. Only the male could retain independence of heart.

The four of them travelled into town in the one jeep, bringing back fleeting images in Lisa's mind of another such night long ago. She had been so young then—so totally ignorant of all the heartache to come. Paul had paid for his mistakes with his life, she only with her memory. Of the two of them, she was the more fortunate in that she had been given the opportunity to redeem herself. Whether Kyle loved her the way she wanted to be loved wasn't important. What mattered was making the best out of this marriage of theirs. A baby, she thought mistily. I want Kyle's child! If she couldn't give him everything she could give him that.

They were welcomed with open arms by the townsfolk, who regarded the Hamilton family as their kith and kin. The cooking itself was done on the beach, while a lively steel band beat out modern pop music as an accompaniment. Dancers in exotic costume performed among the palms. Brought over from Tortola for the occasion, someone said. Children raced everywhere, in and out of the sea, their screams and shouts mingling with the music, with the throbbing of the cicadas to produce a cacophony that hammered at the ears.

'Pure Caribbean!' commented Tod, obviously enjoying the experience. He joined in with enthusiasm when invited to take his turn at the barbecue spits.

'He's gold through and through,' commented Lisa to Madalyn as they watched proceedings from the sidelines. 'A real Texas gentleman!'

'I know. And he's mine for the taking, I know that too.' Madalyn lifted a rueful shoulder. 'I don't love him: it's as simple as that. I only wish I did.'

'Isn't half a loaf better than none?' Lisa murmured, thinking of her own situation.

The snort was derisive. 'That's as bad as "what you never have you never miss"! Don't believe it.' She quietened her tone to add wryly, 'And if I'd half the courage of my convictions I'd take the car and go corner Scott while I have the chance!'

'You may not need to.' Lisa was looking up the beach towards the little sea-front square where they had parked the car. 'Isn't that him just arriving?'

The dark head turned sharply, her expression undergoing a swift and illuminating change. 'Yes, it is.'

'So why not strike while the iron's hot?' suggested Lisa, tongue in cheek, and received a slanting grin.

'"You can lead a horse to water . . ."' She broke off, chin jutting in sudden determination. '"Nothing ventured, nothing gained". He's just going to have to learn to trust again!'

Lisa saw Tod glance up from his cooking as Madalyn made her way towards the man she loved. There was acceptance in his eyes, the look of a man who knew he had lost. Then he was back to turning the sizzling pork chops again, laughing and joking with those surrounding him as if nothing untoward had happened.

Kyle appeared at her elbow bearing a couple of loaded plates. 'Where's Madalyn?' he asked, handing one over. 'I thought she was hungry.'

Lisa nodded towards the square where the two could be seen talking by the second jeep. 'Scott came after all.'

'So I see.' He sounded taut. 'I only hope she knows what she's doing.'

'I think so.' Lisa's voice was soft. 'Scott is the man she wants.'

'Until she gets him.' His lips had twisted. 'Some women are only truly happy when they're unsure of a man.'

'She's your sister,' Lisa protested. 'You must know her better than that!'

The grey eyes held an odd expression. 'I'm not into mind-reading. I only know what she lets me see. Scott was already let down once.'

'I doubt if any marriage break-up is totally one-sided,' she said. 'There have to be faults both sides.' She made a determined effort to lighten the conversation. 'Anyway, they're both adults. They'll sort something out. This pork smells delicious! What's the sauce?'

'An old West Indian recipe.' The lean features were shadowed as he turned his back on the glowing firelight. 'It's supposed to be an aphrodisiac.'

Lisa made herself laugh. 'Does it work?'

'Try it,' he suggested with faint irony, 'and we'll find out.'

Meaning she had need of some extra passion, came the stinging thought, as she concentrated fiercely on the food before her. If he was bored with her already, what chance did they have?

Madalyn did not return to join the party. When the time came to leave, both she and Scott were not to be seen. Neither, Lisa noted, was Scott's jeep.

'Sorry about this,' said Kyle grimly to Tod when the

three of them were in the car. 'That kick in the pants never seemed more apt!'

'The best man won,' returned the other with wry inflection. 'I was more than half expecting it.' There was a pause before he added levelly, 'I'll join you in the morning, if that's OK with you. There's no use in my staying on. I'm not blaming Madalyn for anything. None of us can help the way we feel. She loves this place too much to want to leave it, anyway. Guess it all worked out for the best.'

They drove in near-silence after that. Lisa could feel Kyle's anger simmering inside him. Madalyn had been a little callous, it was true, but that was between her and Tod, no one else. She certainly wouldn't relish interference on her brother's part.

Tod went straight upstairs as soon as they reached the house, refusing Kyle's offer of a night-cap. Viewing the latter's set features as he poured himself a whisky, Lisa knew what inadequacy really felt like.

'Why don't you bring that up with you?' she suggested tentatively when he turned with the glass in his hand. 'It's late, and we have a fairly early start in the morning.'

'If you're tired, you go on up,' he said brusquely. 'I want to see my sister.'

'You'll only say things you're going to regret,' she pleaded. 'Both of you!'

'I'll say what needs saying.' He made a sudden weary little gesture. 'Go to bed, Lisa.'

This doesn't have anything to do with you—the unspoken words rang in her ears. She turned abruptly and left him standing there.

The room she shared with Kyle was at the front of the house. She was brushing her hair by the open window when the jeep drew up outside. There came a murmur of conversation, the sound of someone alighting on to gravel, then the engine revved again and the vehicle moved off, crunching around the turning circle to head back down the drive while Madalyn mounted the veranda steps.

Kyle's voice was muted but still clearly audible on the night air. 'What the hell do you think you're playing at?'

'It's no game,' returned his sister on a level note. 'We decided to give it a try.'

'On the premise that if it doesn't work out you can always try again with someone else?'

'If you mean Tod, he isn't likely to hang around waiting to see,' came the reply. 'All right, so I gave him reason to believe I might marry him. That was a mistake. It would have been an even worse one if I'd done it.'

'Because you're head over heels in love with Scott?' with irony. 'Why now, after three years?'

'It took me a couple to get through the first barriers,' she said. 'The last one only fell tonight when he told me about his wife.'

'Who left him flat, I believe.'

'Who was driven away by his possessiveness, and he's finally acknowledged it to himself.'

'Nicely calculated.'

'Don't preach to me about calculation!' Her voice was harsh. 'You didn't leave much to chance where Lisa's concerned.'

It was a moment or two before the reply came. When Kyle finally spoke it was without inflection. 'I suppose I asked for that.'

'Sat right up and begged for it.' Madalyn's tone altered suddenly, losing its acidity. 'All the same, I shouldn't have said it. Let's leave things alone for tonight, Kyle. We're neither of us in a frame of mind to be fair.'

The semi-silence of a tropical night fell once more as the two of them moved indoors. Lisa stirred herself to finish her brushing, aware that Kyle would be coming through the door in a moment or two. She had learned nothing that she hadn't known already, she told herself dully, so why let it get to her? The onus was still on her to make this marriage work.

It was half an hour or more before he did come up. Lisa was already in bed and feigning sleep. She rolled over with a murmur as he switched on his bedside lamp, opening her eyes slowly as if his movements had awoken her.

'Did Madalyn get back yet?' she asked drowsily.

'Some time ago.' He was peeling off his shirt as he spoke, muscle clearly defined beneath the bronzed skin of his back. 'I've been doing some thinking,' he added. 'Scott can handle things here for a week or two. Why don't we take *Seajade* down through the islands?'

Lisa let out her breath on a faint sigh. She wasn't sure what she had been expecting him to say, except that this wasn't it. 'I'd like that,' she said. 'How soon can we leave?'

He turned to look at her, mouth twisting. 'Day after tomorrow, if you like. I'll have Josh provision her. I should have thought of it sooner.' There was a pause, an indefinable change of expression in the grey eyes. 'Some of our best moments were on board the *Seajade*.'

I know, she wanted to say, but the words stuck in her throat. She put out her arms to him instead, voice husky. 'Come to bed. I think that West Indian recipe is working!'

They landed on St Thomas around two o'clock in the afternoon, transferring to a couple of taxis for the ride out to the airport. Tod and Madalyn had parted on good terms, and he seemed to have accepted the situation philosophically, although Lisa privately thought the hurt had gone a lot deeper than he was letting on. Waving goodbye to him as he exited through passport control, she hoped he wouldn't allow the experience to embitter him against all other women the way Scott had done.

Elaine's flight was called barely half an hour later. She

had told Kyle not to wait but he had insisted. Lisa hung back while mother and son said their goodbyes, unsurprised by the lack of emotion on either side. When it came to her turn she was prepared for the enmity in the pale blue eyes. To Elaine Hamilton she would always be the one responsible for her beloved son's death. Nothing could alter that. It was best for them both that they never meet again.

'I feel as though a ton weight has been lifted,' she confessed to Kyle as they crossed the concourse. 'I know she's your mother . . .'

'Blood ties aren't always the strongest,' he returned evenly. 'She'll be happier where she's going.'

It wouldn't be like that with her children, Lisa silently vowed. She would love them all equally. All? She had to smile. There was a long way to go before she even had one child to think about—although last night might have brought that occasion a step closer. She cast a lingering sideways glance at the lean figure striding at her side, her limbs turning to water at the memory. He had to have some feeling for her to make love with such intensity. And afterwards, holding her so closely in his arms as they drifted off to sleep—as if he wanted to be sure she would be there when he awoke. This time together on *Seajade* was what they needed. Just the two of them alone on the ocean.

'Well, would you look who's here!' The exaggerated American drawl jerked her sharply out of her daydreams. 'The bride and groom, no less!'

It was Kyle who answered, face impassive. 'Hello, Imogen. Leaving or arriving?'

'Meeting, as a matter of fact. My brother.' Her glance skimmed Lisa, the smile perfunctory. 'You seem to have cornered the market in Hamiltons. Let me in on the secret some time.' To Kyle, she added pointedly, 'How did your mother take it?'

He shrugged. 'As might be expected. We just saw her off

to her sister's in Washington.'

'Really?' on a silky note. 'All your problems solved in one fell swoop!'

'You could say that.' Kyle had a hand under Lisa's elbow, his very touch a reassurance. 'Nice seeing you, anyway. Regards to the family.'

Lisa smothered any sense of triumph as they moved on. Imogen had every right to feel bitter. She had lost the man she loved over a piece of land. No matter how one tried to wrap it up, that's what it amounted to.

'Don't let her upset you,' advised Kyle when they were outside and heading for the taxi rank. 'The innuendo was aimed at me.'

'Would you have married her if I hadn't turned up again?' she asked levelly.

The hesitation was brief enough, but it was there. 'It wouldn't have worked out. A couple of days on St Amelia was as much as she could stand.'

'You could always have lived somewhere else.'

'Never. I don't mind a few weeks away from time to time, but it will always be home.' His tone had sharpened. 'I thought you understood that.'

'I do,' she hastened to assure him.

The taxi-driver gave them a friendly grin as they got into the rear seat. 'Where to?'

'The harbour,' Kyle told him. 'No rush.'

'Sure thing.' They had gone only a few yards before he said over a shoulder, 'You folks tourists?'

It was Lisa who answered. 'No, we're islanders.'

'Here?'

'No,' she said again. 'The British group.'

'Well, I guess that's close enough.' He stuck his head out of the opened window to yell at a jaywalking pedestrian, 'You tired of living, man?' bringing it in again to add scathingly, 'Tourist, you bet!'

He kept on talking as he drove, commenting on anything and everything and needing no more than a token murmur from behind to keep him happy. Kyle was looking out of the window, seemingly preoccupied with his own thoughts. Seeing Imogen again had unsettled him, Lisa surmised—perhaps brought home to him just what he had given up. No matter what happened, her shadow would always be there between them. It was a bleak outlook.

They were coming up on a blind bend in the road. Lisa brought her attention to bear on what the man up front was saying as he pointed down to the right.

'Bad smash here a couple of years back. Car hit that tree there—or what's left of it.'

He went on to add something else but she was no longer listening, her gaze fixed on the blackened, twisted trunk. It wasn't dead, she realised. New shoots were sprouting from the charred limbs. Perhaps they'd never be strong, but they were trying.

'Look out, man!' Kyle's shout jerked her head front again to see the truck looming large as it rounded the bend with offside wheels well over the centre line. Too far over himself for safety, their own driver swung his wheel sharply right, hit a layer of loose gravel in the road edge and went into a skidding slide over the rim of the steep incline. To Lisa that bumping, tossing ride seemed to last for ever. She could hear the driver yelling something, saw Kyle reaching out to her as if in slow motion, then she was thrown violently forwards and everything went black.

There was noise and confusion when she opened her eyes again. The sun was bright overhead, the sky limitless in its blueness. Her mind felt amazingly clear and lucid. Apart from a twinge of pain when she moved her head, there seemed to be no damage done. Not to her.

'Kyle!' The name jerked from her lips as she attempted to sit up.

'Don't move. I'm here.' He came into view above her, face drawn. 'The ambulance is on its way.'

'I'm all right,' she said. 'I don't need an ambulance.'

'We'll let the medics decide on that.'

He was kneeling in the grass. Beyond him, Lisa caught a glimpse of the taxi turned on its side. He must have dragged her out through the uppermost door, she realised.

'Thank heaven it didn't catch fire!' she murmured. 'What's all the noise about?'

'Our driver locked in battle with the truck driver,' he told her grimly. 'Sorting out who's to blame before the police get here.'

'So nobody was really hurt?' She gave a small sigh, putting up a shaky hand to trace the streak of dirt down one lean cheek. 'Do you think the same thing might have happened to Paul?'

'I don't know. Right now I don't much care.' He drew in a long breath, eyes fired with determination. 'We've been lucky, Lisa. And we're going to go on being lucky. I thought I'd lost you once—a second time would have killed me!'

She looked at him wonderingly, the knowledge even now only just beginning to seep through. 'You really mean it,' she whispered. 'You really do love me, Kyle?'

Dark brows drew together for a moment. 'Was there ever any doubt?'

'Yes.' She was half laughing, half crying, wincing as the bruise on her forehead made itself known. 'Oh, yes!'

'You're crazy,' he stated. 'Why the devil else would I have put myself through the last few weeks?'

'The island,' she said. 'You wanted St Amelia back.'

'Damn the island. You were what I wanted—what I've always wanted, ever since the day Paul brought you home with him.' His voice was rough. 'You ran away from me once: this time I had to have some hold on you. It was all too quick, I realise that now. I should have given you time to get used to the idea of being married to me.'

'I ran away from you,' she said softly, 'because I loved you too much to bear it when I found out you were only trying to break me and Paul up.'

The strong mouth tautened. 'My mother? I should have known!'

'Then it wasn't true?'

'I might have said something like that in the beginning while I was suffering from deprivation.' He smiled a little. 'I might even have meant it at the time, but if I did it was my own interests I had at heart, not Paul's.' Grey eyes widened suddenly as he realised what she had said. 'You got your memory back!'

'Yes.' There was no need, she thought mistily, to tell him when and why. His mother had been driven by a desire to hurt the way she had been hurt—to make others suffer for the loss of her dearest son. She was out of their lives now, and they had so much catching up to do. The ambulance was coming: she could hear the siren. But it was coming to a beginning this time, not an end.

A TALE OF ILLICIT LOVE

'Defy the Eagle' is a stirring romance set in
Roman Britain at the time of Boadicea's rebellion.
Caddaric is an Iceni warrior loyal to his Queen. The lovely
Jilana is a daughter of Rome and his sworn enemy.
Will their passion survive the hatred of war,
or is the cost too great?
A powerful new novel from Lynn Bartlett.

WORLDWIDE

Price: £3.50   Available: August 1987

Available from Boots, Martins, John Menzies, W.H. Smith,
Woolworths and other paperback stockists.

 **ROMANCE**

Next month's romances from Mills & Boon

Each month, you can choose from a world of variety in romance with Mills & Boon. These are the new titles to look out for next month.

NO ESCAPE Daphne Clair
TOUCH ME IN THE MORNING Catherine George
SUBSTITUTE LOVER Penny Jordan
THE WILDER SHORES OF LOVE Madeleine Ker
ECHO OF PASSION Charlotte Lamb
AN IMPOSSIBLE MAN TO LOVE Roberta Leigh
THE DOUBTFUL MARRIAGE Betty Neels
ENTRANCE TO EDEN Sue Peters
WHERE EAGLES SOAR Emily Spenser
PURE TEMPTATION Sara Wood
*RELUCTANT WIFE Lindsay Armstrong
*MAN SHY Valerie Parv
*SHADOWS Vanessa Grant
*HUSBAND REQUIRED Debbie Macomber

Buy them from your usual paperback stockist, or write to: Mills & Boon Reader Service, P.O. Box 236, Thornton Rd, Croydon, Surrey CR9 3RU, England. Readers in Southern Africa — write to: Independent Book Services Pty, Postbag X3010, Randburg, 2125, S. Africa.

*These four titles are available from Mills & Boon Reader Service.

Mills & Boon
the rose of romance

ACCEPT 4
MILLS & BOON
ROMANCES
ABSOLUTELY FREE

...after all, what better way to continue your enjoyment of the finest stories from the world's foremost romantic authors? This is a very special introductory offer designed for regular readers. Once you've read your four **free** books you can take out a subscription (although there's no obligation at all). Subscribers enjoy many special benefits and all these are described overleaf. ▶▶▶

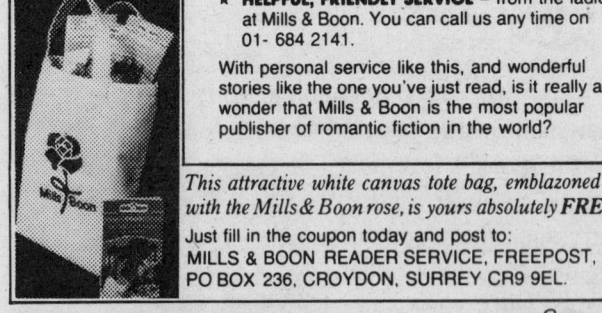